FOWL PLAY

After their spaceship crashed on Earth (Newman was driving), John Newman and Jim Halligan took the only course of action available to aliens stranded on this planet. They became teachers.

Having drunk the last of their rocket fuel, they turned to writing. Their first efforts were the much-loathed schoolbooks *Simply Science, Try This* and *A Way With Words*, which turned our two heroes into hate figures across the nation.

Their first two efforts at children's fiction, *Fowl Play* and *Round the Bend*, made the two geniuses household names in lunatic asylums all over the planet. *Fowl Deeds* was an attempt to attract the attention of a really good psychiartrist.

After spending years in therapy they've now decided they're lost causes and have written their new epic – *Seeing Red*, which could destroy the world in Spring 2003.

ALSO BY JIM HALLIGAN AND JOHN NEWMAN

Round the Bend (1999)

Fowl Deeds (2000)

Coming Soon...

Seeing Red (2003)

FOWL PLAY

Jim Halligan
and
John Newman

Illustrated by
Aileen Caffrey

WOLFHOUND PRESS

First published in 1998 by
WOLFHOUND PRESS
An imprint of Merlin Publishing
16 Upper Pembroke Street
Dublin 2
Ireland
publishing@merlin.ie
www.merlin-publishing.com

Reprinted 2003

Text Copyright © 2000 Jim Halligan and John Newman

ISBN 0-86327-639-3

A CIP catalogue record for this book is available
from the British Library.

10 9 8 7 6 5 4 3 2

Cover Illustration by Aileen Caffery
Cover Design by Aileen Caffery/Reprolink
Typeset by Wolfhound Press
Printed by Cox & Wyman Ltd

For Astrid and Jane

PROLOGUE

T wo huddled figures trudged through the grey, damp mist of a November afternoon. The quiet country road always seemed twice its usual length on days like this. School had been stuffy and boring. Homework and the usual daily chores of the farm awaited them. At least they were nearly home.

The old house to their left was the last one before their own farm. Its high, forbidding walls loomed above them out of the mist as they walked silently along. The old signs hung, as usual, on the walls and on the huge, closed iron gate:

PRIVATE PROPERTY

KEEP OUT

NO TRESPASSERS

What was behind those walls with the broken glass cemented on top? No one knew. Old Miller seldom came to the village. He ordered what he wanted by telephone and it was left at the gate. Once a month, he ventured into Narrowview to pay his bills. That was all anyone knew about him.

Of course, everyone had his or her own opinion. Some said that he was a retired gangster. Others swore he was a mad inventor. The more imaginative claimed that he was a terrible murderer who had changed his identity to escape the law. Few people ever saw him, and even fewer had ever spoken to him.

Sometimes the two children would play guessing games about Old Miller's past. But this day was too wet and dull and grey; they walked along without any chatter.

Just as they passed the old gates, they heard a grating, creaking noise. Both heads turned towards the sound.

No more than seven steps away, Old Miller stared intently at the two children. He did not make a sound. He just looked .

All the wild images from those guessing games came rushing into the children's heads. They turned and ran ....

Chapter One

The Hooray Henery Chicken Farm nestled beside the Miller place in a sleepy valley outside the village of Narrowview. It was a noisy, carefree place by day; but now, as night drew to an end, its six hundred chickens, one dog and four humans slept soundly.

A cock strutted across the dim farmyard. He fluttered up onto the seat of a rusty tractor and checked the horizon.

A thin line of light could be seen on the hills to the east. The cock stretched out his scrawny neck and proudly, loudly, announced the new day.

'Cock-a-doodle-doo! Cock-a-doodle-doo-oo-oo!' he screeched.

'Oh, hell!' muttered Terry, and buried her head deep under her pillow.

In the bed opposite her, Alex swung his legs out from under the sheets and sat up. He allowed himself one stretch and then reached for his handkerchief. He unfolded it carefully and, taking his glasses from his bedside table, he cleaned them thoroughly before placing them on his face.

The room swam into focus and, as so often before, Alex was greeted by the distressing sight of his twin sister's half of the room.

'Terry, it is 6.45 a.m. Time to rise,' he told the heap of

quilt which presumably hid his twin.

'Ooooh, no!' moaned Terry from far, far away. 'I can't move. I'm dead!'

'Terry, you can move and you are not dead,' explained Alex. 'Now, rise and shine.'

'Ah, go and jump in the lake,' muttered Terry crossly, into her pillow.

'Get up NOW, Terry!' shouted their father as he passed the bedroom door on his way from the bathroom, a blob of shaving cream still on his chin. Terry groaned loudly.

Alex straightened his tie, tucked in his shirt and, with his big toe, deftly pushed a pair of Terry's socks across the floor to her side of the room. He could already hear Rags throwing himself at the back door as Mrs Patterson drew back the bolt and pulled the door open.

'Ready, steady … go!' mouthed Alex, and clicked his stopwatch.

'Easy, Rags!' laughed his mother as the dog tore past her.

'… Three, four, five seconds,' Alex counted as Rags skidded, yelping, across the flagstoned floor of the kitchen.

'… Six, seven, eight.' Rags took the stairs two steps at a time.

'… Nine and ten,' Alex finished, as the dog crashed past him and took a flying leap at Terry's bed.

'Down, Rags, down!' shouted Terry.

Rags licked her face. 'Get off, you great lump!' she yelled, laughing. Rags dragged the quilt off her with his teeth. Lunging at the dog, Terry grabbed him by his matted hair and they both tumbled, yelping, onto the floor.

Alex picked a dog hair off his trouser leg and looked at his wreck of a sister.

She had obviously slept in her clothes; they were a crinkled mess. There was straw in her hair and she had been eating blackberries in bed again.

'You could at least have taken off your shoes, Terry,' he said as he asked himself, for perhaps the thousandth time, whether this could really be his twin.

It was still quite dark and cold when the twins set about collecting the morning eggs before heading off to school. Terry was still half asleep. Her coat was buttoned up wrongly and she stumbled along.

'My feet hurt,' she complained, 'and I want to go back to bed.'

Alex glanced at his sister. It was not like her to whinge.

'It's your boots again, Terry,' he explained kindly. 'They're on the wrong feet.'

Terry sighed as she pulled off her boots. Alex sighed, too, noticing her big toes poking out of both socks. He pulled on the white glove he always used when collecting eggs, and urged his sister to hurry up.

'It is 7.23 a.m. and we haven't started yet!'

The twins spent the next half-hour trailing about the yard, searching out the hidey-holes where the hens usually laid their eggs. Alex was doing well; his bucket was nearly full.

Terry, however, was making slow progress, which was not like her. Normally she would race around the yard, whooping every time she found an egg, greeting each hen by name, teasing them if they hadn't laid, congratulating them if they had.

'What an enormous egg, Alice 19,' she'd shout. 'That must have hurt!'

'Maria, Maria 43, you haven't laid again. I think you're lovesick,' she'd tease the shy brown bantam. 'Is it Roger Rooster you've fallen feather over claw for?' And she would gently squeeze the hen's beak between her fingers.

Terry had an enviable way with hens. She loved them and they loved her. But today, instead of getting on with collecting their eggs, she was sadly hugging each hen in turn.

Alex tried to jolly her up. 'How about trying egg-juggling again, Terry?' he called, stepping over his father's legs and starting to search the trailer.

Mr Patterson was already at work under the tractor; all that could be seen of him was his lower half, stretched out across the dirty yard. He was muttering and cursing to himself. Rags, as usual, was wrestling with the front wheel of the tractor.

Terry sighed.

'Not today, Alex. I can't help thinking about poor old Mildred 7,' she answered sadly.

'What about her?' asked Alex, puzzled.

'She hasn't laid an egg for weeks,' said Terry, close to tears, 'and today is Biddle Day!'

Biddle Day? Surely not! Alex wouldn't have forgotten that — would he?

He frowned. Putting down his bucket of eggs, he pulled his filofax out of his coat pocket and started flicking through it.

'Thursday, Thursday ... Thursday 10 November. 11.00 a.m. — Biddle.'

Terry was right! Alex frowned deeply. How had he forgotten? Was this a once-off, never-to-be-repeated memory lapse, or did it indicate something more serious? Was he ill?

'Biddle Day!' moaned Terry, so sadly that Alex forgot about his own worries. With a heavy heart, he took both their buckets and carried them to his mother in the kitchen.

As the twins left the yard that fateful morning on their way to school, a sense of foreboding settled over the normally happy Hooray Henery Chicken Farm.

It was Thursday 10 November. It was Biddle Day.

Chapter Two

Mildred 7 was the oldest hen on the Hooray Henery Chicken Farm. Like all of the Pattersons' hens, she had been given her name by Terry and her number by Alex (Alex liked to keep things in order). She was the seventh hen to bear the name 'Mildred'. The six Mildreds before her had all ended up taking that last fatal trip in Sam Biddle's blue van.

But there was something different about Mildred 7. All of the other hens had much higher numbers than she, such as 'Alice 19' or 'Henrietta 23'. This was no mere coincidence. Mildred 7 was a natural-born survivor. Her great talent was an ability to make herself scarce whenever she heard the well-tuned engine of Sam Biddle's blue van making its way up the farm lane.

Maybe she was even able to tell when it was Biddle Day. Whatever her secret, Mildred 7 had lasted longer than any other hen on the farm, and that suited her just fine. So, whenever Griselda 24 and Juliette 18 and all the others headed off in the blue van to become chicken stock cubes, you could be sure that Mildred 7 wouldn't be going with them if she could help it.

It must have been old age, but on this particular Biddle Day, Mildred 7 had been caught napping.

It came as quite a shock to her to look up from her

pecking and see the majestic blue van come to a halt in the farmyard.

It was definitely time for a bit of quick thinking and running.

Now, running was not a thing that the other hens associated with Mildred 7. She normally strutted around the farm slowly and deliberately, with great dignity. Right now, she was flitting along like a four-week-old chick with a good wind at her back.

Something was definitely wrong.

Some of the other birds became edgy too. Maybe the big blue thing in the yard meant trouble. Where was Mildred 7 going? And why?

They decided to follow her example. Soon every hen in the yard was running after Mildred — even Roger the rooster. All in all, it looked like a kind of chicken marathon, with Mildred 7 very much in the lead.

She ran frantically from one hiding-place to another. Her first choice was the old water trough. The entire flock of hens followed her. Well, that was no good. She moved on to choice number two, the old tree-stump by the fence, but they followed her there too. No matter where she ran, the others would spoil the hiding-place. The whole stampede had stopped looking like a chicken marathon; now it seemed more like a chicken treasure hunt. Mildred 7 looked like the one with all the clues, and all the others were following her.

She was becoming desperate. There was no way she could escape from the rest of the flock. There was no-where on the farm she could hide them all .... Nowhere on the farm ....

That was it!

The flock of frantic poultry had reached the edge of their known world. Ahead of them lay the patch of brambles which marked the boundary of the Hooray Henery Farm. To their right was the road. To their left ran the river. They were desperate, not stupid. The brambles it was.

Through the brambles they dashed, until they reached the high wall of the Miller place. As luck would have it, Mildred 7 and her flock of desperadoes found a hole in the wall. They piled through it.

Sam Biddle, the source of Mildred 7's terror, stepped down from his magnificent blue van. He ran his hand along its polished paintwork. It gleamed. Sam Biddle's van might be used for hauling luckless chickens around the countryside, but it was always spotless. He pampered it like a spoiled child. It had been his best friend for years. He loved his van, and his love for it showed.

It must be said that the van was in much better condition than Sam Biddle was. In fact, at the best of times, he was not a pretty sight. Years before, he had been a compact, athletic man; now he was short and fat. His once-keen eyes were bloodshot and watery behind thick glasses. He always managed to have a three-day-old stubble of beard on his chin.

You could easily have loved a man with these features if he had been kind. But Sam Biddle was a mean man. He really loved only two things — his blue van, and killing chickens.

Killing chickens was what Biddle Day was all about. Sam Biddle would travel around the countryside visiting all of the poultry farms. Any chickens which were no longer able to lay eggs ended up in the back of his blue van. After that, they might find themselves (or parts of themselves) in some butcher's window. That, or they could go to the chicken-stock-cube factory. The plumpest chickens Biddle would always keep for himself.

'I particularly enjoy their livers,' he had lisped at Terry, once, in his thick-tongued voice. He knew it would upset her.

This time, as Biddle stood in the near-deserted farmyard, there was no Terry to upset. Neither, for that matter, were there any chickens to put in the van. The day was not going according to plan.

Still, there was always the dog.

Sam Biddle aimed a kick at Rags, who deftly ran out of the way.

Sighing his disappointment, Biddle shuffled over to Mr Patterson, who still lay grumbling under the tractor.

'Patterson,' he lisped.

Mr Patterson, still absorbed by a festering wound in the tractor's innards, grunted half-heartedly.

'Patterson!' lisped Sam Biddle, again.

The twins' father, thinking about major surgery on the tractor's gearbox, carried on with what he was doing beneath the machine. An oily hand reached out past one of the large black tyres, fumbled around, grasped a socket wrench and retreated back beneath the stricken vehicle.

'PATTERSON!!' howled the red-faced Sam Biddle.

'Wha ...?' Clunk! Mr Patterson had made the serious mistake of sitting bolt upright while still under his tractor. There had been a collision between head and metal. Metal had won. The twins' father — still hidden from view, apart from his legs — moaned softly.

'Look,' spluttered the indignant Sam Biddle, 'I come all the way out to this godforsaken farm of yours to pay you good money for a few of your scrawny chickens.

And what happens? Eh? I see the whole lot of 'em high-tail it out of sight.'

He ran the back of his hand over his wet chin and continued. 'It's just not good enough. You could at least have them ready for me to collect. Instead, what do I get? Eh? I'll tell you — I get the run-around!'

There was another moan ....

'I don't care what you say. I've got a business to run.'

Then a grunt ....

'I'll be back this afternoon. You'd better have those chickens ready.'

Mr Patterson slowly, painfully pushed himself out from underneath the tractor. Somehow, he had gone right off the idea of fixing it.

'By the way, you seem to have a bump on your forehead. It's not wise to work on machinery if you're not in proper health; you might hurt yourself. Till this afternoon, then.'

Sam Biddle turned, aimed another unsuccessful kick at Rags, got into his van and drove off.

Mr Patterson sat quietly in the farmyard for a little while before going into the house to look for some ice.

Chapter Three

Terry hurried along, pulling her schoolbag on the ground after her.

'Watch out for that puddle,' warned Alex breathlessly, struggling to keep up with her.

But Terry paid him no heed; she dragged her tattered bag through the brown puddles which had formed in the deep potholes along the lane to the Hooray Henery Chicken Farm.

'It's very quiet,' she commented. 'Come on, hurry up!'

Alex *was* hurrying, but there was no point in getting mud all over his school shoes, was there? The laneway was a disgrace — more like a network of small craters than a road. Oh for smooth jet-black tarmac, he thought, tiptoeing through a particularly muddy patch.

Terry was right. The farmyard was very quiet indeed. There was an eerie silence which stopped both children in their tracks.

Except for their father, cursing quietly underneath the tractor, there was absolutely no sound.

'The hens!' shouted Terry. 'Biddle's taken all the hens!'

She flung down her schoolbag and rushed over to the tractor. Her face was white with anger.

'Where are they?' she shouted at her father — who, taken by surprise, lifted his head and belted it, for the second time that day, off the underside of the tractor.

'Aaaannh ....' he moaned, but Terry was having none of it. She grabbed his ankles and hauled him out from beneath the machine. His shirt was up around his armpits and his face was covered in oil.

'You let Biddle take them all!' she yelled. She leapt on the poor man, pummelling his chest with her fists. Tears poured down her face. 'How could you? How could you?'

'I didn't! I didn't!' Mr Patterson shouted back, trying to shield himself, especially his bandaged head, from her blows. He was too surprised at the ferocity of her attack to do the proper, fatherly thing and roar at her.

Alex finally puffed into the yard.

'Pull yourself together, Terry!' he commanded. 'Let Father speak before you go jumping to conclusions. There may be a rational explanation for the disappearance of the poultry.' But, for the life of him, he couldn't think of one.

Terry stopped thumping her father. Her hair had fallen over her face and her eyes were red.

'Well, Father, what do you have to say in your defence?' continued Alex in the same serious tone.

'Oh, the hens are gone, all right,' said their father with a sigh. His head really hurt.

'I told you,' snarled Terry to her brother, clenching her fists again. But Mr Patterson was not going to be caught twice.

'But Biddle hasn't got them!' he bellowed, heaving his daughter off his chest.

'Oh!' said Terry, speechless for once.

'And whereabouts might they be?' asked Alex, as his father scuttled back to the relative peace and quiet beneath the tractor.

'They all scarpered when Biddle came,' Mr Patterson called out to them. 'And it's up to you two to go and find them — NOW!'

As it happened, Sam Biddle was not very far away. He was standing in the roadway, less than a minute from the Pattersons' farm, spluttering curses to himself. His beautiful blue van, his pride and joy, which he had only polished that very morning, was in a bit of a state.

Long streaks of cow dung smeared its classically curved side-panels. Its elegantly styled bonnet was splattered with mud. Sam Biddle's eyes bulged. His face reddened. A shower of spittle sprayed from his lips as he roundly cursed the Hooray Henery Chicken Farm and all its filthy potholes. After that morning's disaster, those chickens had better be there!

'Dirty, filthy, manky farm!' he spat, as he wiped the van with his huge, spotty handkerchief before the dung could become completely encrusted on the lovely bodywork.

In his rage, he almost didn't notice Terry and Alex running across the river field, chasing that fleabag mongrel of theirs.

'Hurry up, Alex,' he heard the dreadful girl shout.

'Horrible, filthy creature,' muttered Sam Biddle, wiping his nose with his spotty handkerchief.

'Rags will lead us to the chickens!' she yelled, laughing and jumping about in that ridiculous way of hers.

Sam Biddle stuffed the handkerchief into his pocket, wiped his hands on the back of his trousers and let a slow, ugly leer spread across his face.

'And you, my filthy child, will lead *me* to those chickens,' he crowed. He set off after the children.

They were quite a bit ahead of him, and they were moving faster than he could. Biddle tore the backside out of his trousers as he climbed the gate into the river field.

'Damn kids ... should be gutted ....' he grunted, as he started across the grass. The whole place was water-logged, and with each step he sank into oozing mud up to his ankles.

By the time he reached the far side of the field and found the gap in the brambles through which the children had disappeared, Sam Biddle was in a royal bad mood. His face was the shade of an overripe tomato, and his breath came in great gulps. It had been a very long time since he had run anywhere, and he was exhausted.

Hitching up his trousers, he charged like a demented bull through the gap in the hedge. But the brambles seemed to have it in for Sam Biddle. They tore at his arms; they gripped at his shirt; they ripped his legs and scratched his face. Still, he battled on. He burst out of the brambles just in time to see the children disappear through another hole — this time in a high, forbidding, glass-topped wall.

But Sam Biddle was a determined man. Once he had the scent, he didn't give up easily. So, although he was wheezing and spluttering like a broken-down old steam engine, he once again set off in pursuit of the children ... and those nice plump chickens.

Terry, who was very acrobatic and agile, had easily
slipped through the narrow hole in the wall, and was
helping Alex to squeeze himself through.

'We're in the Miller place,' she said, in a low voice.

'And that means we are trespassing. We must leave
immediately or face certain prosecution,' declared a
horrified Alex, brushing dirt off his trouser leg.

'Yeah, right,' muttered Terry, ignoring her brother.
Then she tensed and pointed. 'Look,' she hissed. 'There
they are.'

Sure enough, there was the entire flock of hens,
huddled beneath a huge tree. Their feathers were
puffed up and their heads were held low. There was a
determined and defiant air about them. Every few
moments one or two heads would pop up, as members
of the flock recognised the twins.

'This is a strange orchard,' commented Alex, looking
around at the trees. 'These are all walnut trees .... Most
peculiar!'

Rags shivered and tucked his tail between his legs.

'What's up, fella?' asked Terry, rubbing the dog's
head.

'It's this place,' said Alex. 'It's strange. We should
take the hens and go.'

'And go do our homework?' taunted his sister.
'Alex, get a life! We'll never get a chance like this again.
Just a *little* look around?'

Alex didn't like it, but he was curious — very curious.
He had always been puzzled by the Miller place. Why
was it always shut up? Why did they never really see
Old Miller? Why were there no animals on the farm?
He didn't believe the scaremongering rumours that
went around the village — but he had a few theories of
his own ....

Alex didn't like the idea of poking about uninvited, but this was too good a chance to miss.

'Five minutes, max, and then we go!' he told his sister.

The hens watched the two children and Rags suspiciously as the three of them made their way through the walnut orchard and crept towards a large open yard ringed by old, rusty barns. Grass pushed its way through the broken cement of the yard; the place looked as though it had been abandoned for years.

As the children stood and considered their next move, neither of them noticed the shadowy figure watching silently from an upper window of the sombre grey house which took up one side of the deserted yard.

'Let's look in here,' whispered Terry, pulling at the door of the nearest barn.

'That's breaking and entering,' snapped Alex crossly. Then he helped his sister to drag the rusted door open.

In the meantime, Sam Biddle had reached the wall. He leaned his back against it and tried to catch his breath. His great belly swelled and fell as he gulped air in large lungfuls. His crimson face was drenched with sweat. There was no way on earth he was going to get through that hole in the wall. He could peer through it — perhaps even push his head through it — but that was about it. He'd have to scale the wall if he was to get inside.

Using the hole as a foothold, Biddle heaved himself up the side of the wall. His fingers felt carefully at the top for glass — good, there was hardly any. Now to

pull himself up .... With a mighty effort he pulled his
elbow onto the top of the wall, his legs dangling in
mid-air, the backside of his torn trousers flapping in the
breeze. He could feel his heart beating wildly in his
considerable bulk as he hung over the wall.

Sam Biddle might have come to the end of his
strength, but he could at least see the chickens ... and
those blasted kids!

'What are they up to now?' he muttered to himself,
as he watched them pull open the barn door. 'Little
thugs — should be horsewhipped!'

He could also see a figure coming out of the house.
'Must be Miller,' he thought. Biddle had heard stories
about him — he was a serial killer or a mass murderer
or something. Clearly, the kids were unaware of his
approach.

A thought crossed Sam Biddle's mind. He should
shout a warning to them .... But then again, perhaps
not! The world would be well rid of those two.

The figure was moving stealthily towards Alex and
Terry. Biddle could hardly contain his excitement.

But what in the name of goodness was that coming
out of the barn? It was some kind of turkey — or was
it? It was a strange, ugly-looking bird. It walked towards
the children, its head cocked to one side.

Sam Biddle had never seen a bird like it — and he
certainly knew his fowl!

Neither Terry nor Alex knew what to make of it
either. Rags cowered behind their legs. And more of the
strange creatures were walking out of the barn towards
the baffled children. The children stared at the birds.
The birds stared back at the twins.

Alex took a step backwards. Terry took a step forwards.

'They are so ugly!' said Alex.

'They are so cute!' said Terry, slowly approaching the first bird.

That was when Sam Biddle fell off the wall. His gargling howl was followed by a thump as he landed in a clump of nettles .... Then there was more howling.

The twins, startled, swung around. The tall, thin, grey form of Old Miller stood behind them, his hand raised and his mouth half open.

Terry screamed. Rags bolted. Alex grabbed his sister's hand and fled after the dog.

Back through the trees they ran, as fast as their legs could carry them.

'Wait!' shouted the old man behind them.

They ran faster, with the speed and determination which only truly terrified people can achieve. The chickens, already edgy after their upset of the morning, sensed further danger and joined in, squawking and squabbling and flapping all over the place.

The children had almost reached the wall — Rags was already scrambling through the hole — when, WHOOOOOSH! Suddenly they were both lifted off the ground and swung, legs first, into the air.

Chapter Four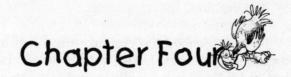

The twins were swinging upside down in a large net. The world seemed to be swaying gently above their heads. In any other circumstances, Terry would certainly and Alex would probably have enjoyed the experience. But they were in enemy territory — and helpless.

'They say he eats kids, Alex.'

'Doubt it, Terry.'

Rags looked at them from the ground below — or above, from the twins' point of view. Mildred 7 and her flock of renegades still held their ground under some of the further-away walnut trees.

A pair of booted feet approached. Each footstep made a rustling noise on the ground. With each step, the twins' heartbeats grew faster. Their hearts were pounding by the time the steps ceased.

'Soon have you down,' a voice gently assured them.

The twins realised exactly whose feet those were. All the wild rumours about Old Miller rushed through their minds. Terry had believed every one of them. Alex had argued logically that they could not possibly be true. Now, both of them screamed.

'We're going to be mass-murdered!' yelled Terry.

The net started to move gently back towards the ground.

'Calm down, children. No one is going to harm you.

Let's get you out of this dog trap.'

Alex regained his composure.

'Dog trap?'

The net touched the ground. Arms, legs and heads were deftly untangled. Alex quickly tidied himself back into order. Terry had actually looked better upside down.

They faced the old man.

'Sorry, did you say "dog trap"?' asked Alex.

'That's right,' replied Old Miller. 'I need to keep cats, dogs and rats away from my buildings. With nets like this all over the grounds, I can catch them before they do any harm and then let them go.'

The 'let them go' bit sounded promising.

'You mean you're not a mass murderer?' asked Terry.

'I'm afraid not,' smiled the old man. 'Why? Are you disappointed?'

'NO!' squeaked the twins together.

'Most dogs from around here have spent a little time in my nets. Isn't that right, Rags?' he asked the dog.

Rags slouched over to Terry and licked her hand in his best 'Well, I tried to warn you' way.

Alex's sense of good manners kicked into action. 'Er, I'm Alex Patterson and this is my twin sister, Terry.' He offered a grimy hand.

'Professor Aidan Miller.' The old man formally accepted the handshake.

'Professor ....' Alex began to think that here might be a person who could share his precise view of the world.

Terry hadn't said a word, which was odd for her. In fact, she seemed to be in a trance. She stared straight past Alex and Professor Miller, towards the barns. Her eyes were locked on the strange birds. It was the first chance she had had to see them properly; and something was very definitely amiss here.

The birds, about forty or fifty in all, were approaching. They seemed curious rather than frightened. There was something in the way they moved which made them appear more intelligent than the chickens, even Mildred 7. Their yellow eyes seemed so ... so calm and trusting.

Heaven knew, they weren't much to look at. In fact, they looked downright ridiculous — something like an unlucky pigeon crossed with an even more unlucky turkey.

They were huge. Their heads nearly came up to Terry's shoulder. Their feathers were a dull, stony grey. Each bird had a pair of hopelessly stubby wings, and a sad little feathery plume for a tail. A bare, pink face ended in an elongated parrot-type beak, the sort of thing that looked like it could open bottles — but very badly. The whole concoction stood on two stout, sturdy, giant chicken legs.

'What are they?' asked Terry, in a voice barely above a whisper (not her style at all).

'Ah ... you have discovered my secret,' the Professor said. 'If you'd like to come into the house, I'll try to explain. First, let's get them back into the bird shed.'

Silently nodding once to each other, the twins followed the Professor.

Professor Miller's house was a magical place. It was dark and smelled of old leather, and its walls were lined with books. There were more books piled on tables, and even some stacked on the floor. Where there weren't books, there were glass cases. The ordinary furniture of the house squeezed in here and there as best it could.

The old man watched patiently as Alex inspected the rows, stacks and piles of books. Terry moved thoughtfully from glass case to glass case. Some cases displayed rows of large eggs; others held dried leaves and peculiar-looking nuts; still more contained stuffed examples of the strange birds outside. There were also maps and, in one case, on its own, a large, battered, leather-bound book.

After a few silent minutes, both children looked at Professor Miller. He gestured to an old leather sofa and they both sat down.

'I'm afraid I'm at your mercy,' he said.

The twins looked puzzled.

'I need you to tell absolutely no one about what you've seen here today. No one,' he emphasised. 'Do you think you can keep this a secret?'

'I don't think we really understand,' said Terry. Alex nodded.

'The birds you have just seen are the only ones of their kind in the whole world.'

'You mean they're some kind of new breed?' asked Alex.

'No. Quite the opposite. They are a very old breed. In fact, as far as the rest of the world knows, they are extinct.'

'They're dodos, aren't they?' Terry's voice was calm.

'Yes, my dear, they are.'

'But that's impossible!' blurted Alex.

'Obviously not,' said the Professor. 'You have seen them. They are very much alive ... and I will need your help to keep them alive.' His eyes were imploring. 'Perhaps I should tell you the whole story ....'

'More than three hundred years ago,' the Professor began, 'an ancestor of mine, Thomas Miller, sailed as a navigator on board a Portuguese trading ship. The voyage he made on that ship was to affect not only his own life but the lives of his descendants ever since.

'During the voyage, the ship visited the island of Mauritius in the Indian Ocean. It was a popular spot for sailors to take on fresh water and food.

'Mauritius was the home of the dodo birds. They were easy to catch and kill for meat. By the time Thomas Miller's ship arrived, there were only a handful of dodos left.'

The Professor paused, walked over to a glass case and removed the large, battered book which Terry had noticed. He opened the book for them.

'This tells the whole story. Thomas Miller witnessed the death of the last dodo. The sailors made a great celebration of it. He was horrified.

'But as luck would have it, the last few dodos had just nested. Thomas Miller decided to collect the eggs. He found seven nests, each one containing a single egg; the parent birds had all been killed by his shipmates for food. Thomas Miller decided there and then to try to keep the eggs safe and allow the chicks to hatch.

'It still strikes me as a miracle that all seven eggs hatched on the voyage home. Those seven chicks, four hens and three cocks, were the only survivors of the slaughter.

'Thomas vowed to raise the chicks and try to breed them secretly. He hoped that, someday, he or his children would be able to bring the dodos back to Mauritius. Saving the birds became an obsession for him — one which was passed on to every generation of the family which followed.'

Alex frowned.

'Why did it all have to happen in secret?' he asked.

'Well ....' The Professor rubbed his chin. 'Rare things take on a value of their own. Thomas Miller realised that if word of the dodos got out, they would be treated like some kind of sideshow. What the birds needed was peace and quiet to breed and increase their numbers. Through the years, ever since the time of Thomas Miller, the survival of the dodos has been a secret mission for my family.'

'Thomas never got a chance to bring the dodos back, did he?' asked Terry.

'No. Dodos are very difficult to breed in captivity. That's why there are so few, even today. Thomas Miller died without ever having enough dodos to take back to the island. It is just as well that he didn't.'

'Why?' asked Alex. 'Surely their native island was the best place for them to live?'

'There was still danger from sailors, right?' said Terry.

'Well, yes. But there was a more serious problem than that. We now know that it wasn't just humans who did the damage, back in Thomas Miller's day. Rats, cats and dogs had been let loose on the island. They killed chicks and destroyed eggs. The very same thing could happen now. Mauritius is no longer a safe place for dodos.'

'But then you'll never be able to release your dodos into the wild.'

The Professor beckoned the children over to a large map on the wall.

'We have solved that problem,' he said. 'What was needed was another island, with the same conditions and plant types as Mauritius. My grandfather found and bought a remote island in the Indian Ocean which will be a perfect home for the birds. He even managed to plant it with the trees and other plants which the dodos depend on for food. Miller Island is their only hope for the future. And they will have to go soon.' The Professor smiled. 'I'm not as young as I used to be. I am also the last of the Millers.'

'Couldn't we help?' asked Terry. 'We could carry stuff — help feed them .... I mean, I'm good with chickens ....'

'She's the best,' declared Alex proudly. 'She really knows how to handle birds.' He paused. 'I'm good with paperwork,' he said brightly.

'So long as you tell no one else ....' warned the Professor.

'Wouldn't dream of it!'

'No way!'

'Well, then,' Professor Miller said, rubbing his hands and smiling, 'it appears that the dodos have two new friends.'

He looked at his watch. 'Your parents will be beginning to worry about you. Don't you have your chickens to round up?'

'You're right,' admitted Alex, 'we'd better be getting along. C'mon, Terry.'

As the pair headed for the door, Terry turned to the old man.

'Listen, is there any chance we could leave one of our chickens here with you?'

'Of course, but why?' enquired the Professor.

'It's Mildred 7,' explained Terry. 'She's an old hen that we're both very fond of, and I'd say Biddle will take her if she comes back to the farm with us.' Alex nodded solemnly.

'She's more than welcome to stay,' Professor Miller assured them. 'I'd be glad of the company.'

'Well, if it's company you want, we'll be happy to come over and help you, won't we, Ter?' said Alex.

'You would be most welcome. In fact, if you are lucky, you'll see my last dodo egg hatching. It's due sometime near the end of this week.'

'That'd be great!' Both twins beamed.

'Right — till tomorrow, then. I'll give you a proper tour of the dodo house and explain how they are cared for.'

Minutes later, Mildred 7 was watching her fellow chickens troop back through the hole in the wall towards the Hooray Henery Chicken Farm. She didn't envy them one bit.

As they made their way through the brambles, neither the chickens nor the twins noticed the trampled patch where Sam Biddle had been.

Chapter Five

In the crowded dining room of Marcel La Bouche's restaurant, La Grande Bouche, smartly dressed people oohed and aahed over plates of complicated-looking food. Waiters swiftly and smoothly placed dishes on crisp white tablecloths. In the soft lighting of the beautifully decorated room, diamonds glittered on wrists and necks.

An Italian opera was being played quietly through the expensive loudspeakers hidden in the ceiling. From those loudspeakers, a lady was singing about how she had dashed out the evil count's brains with a sledge-hammer to save the man she loved from being boiled alive in hot oil. Fortunately, nobody in the room under-stood the words. They thought the music was fabulous.

Everyone thought that the food was fabulous too. This was probably just as well, because it cost a fortune. Marcel La Bouche was a world-famous chef, and he charged world-famous prices.

From his seat in a quiet corner of the restaurant, a young man called over the head waiter.

'Yes, sir?'

'Hi, I was wondering if I could have some tomato ketchup, please?'

The waiter turned pale and instantly headed for the door leading to the kitchen.

Seconds later, that same door burst open, and out thundered a furious Marcel La Bouche.

His tall, elegant figure filled the doorway. Marcel was a man who knew how to look impressive in any situation. His perfectly cut dark hair was slicked back beneath his snow-white chef's hat. His white chef's uniform looked as though it had been made by a master tailor (which, in fact, it had). A pencil-thin moustache sat on the upper lip of his perfectly tanned face. Marcel used good looks and charm like a shark uses its teeth.

Right now, he was hopping mad.

'Where is he?' he shrieked. 'Where is this — this *peasant* who ordered *to-ma-to ketch-up*?' He spat out the words.

'I ... well, I ....' The young man who had ordered the ketchup felt like something at the wrong end of a microscope — very, very small.

'So it is you!' Marcel glared at him down the length of his elegant nose.

'Well, if it's OK, I'd ... um ....'

'No, it is *not* OK, sonny! *Nobody* comes into *my* restaurant looking for cheap sauces!' Marcel knew he was winning. This was so easy! Every other conversation in the room had withered and died. Somewhere in the ceiling, the Italian opera singer was describing how the evil count's head had caved in; but nobody was paying any attention to her now. All eyes were on Marcel.

The young man made one last effort to defend himself.

'Well, look ....'

Big mistake. Marcel cut him off.

'I laboured! I sweated! I *slaved* in that kitchen so that you could taste the best food in the world. And now you want to pour sloppy, icky squashed tomatoes all over it?'

'Um ... ah ....'

Another victory for Marcel La Bouche!

'Get out! Get out of my restaurant! You must have the taste buds of a hedgehog. Get out and never come back!'

The other diners stared open-mouthed at Marcel, like a flock of sheep watching a wolf in action. Marcel glared at them.

'Anyone else? Any more bog-trotters? I believe there's a fast-food burger joint somewhere in town .... Eh? Eh?'

The flock of nervous diners returned their attention to the food in front of them. The oohing and aahing began again in earnest.

'That's better,' growled Marcel. 'Now get on with it!' He stormed back to his kitchen.

Meanwhile, back in the ceiling, the lady's voice warbled on in Italian about how the evil count's eyeballs had rolled down the mountainside and caused an avalanche which wiped out her entire village. Well, that's tragic opera.

In his office, at the back of his kitchen, Marcel calmed down and thumbed his way through a nature magazine.

He was very interested in endangered species of wild birds and animals.

Actually, he was very interested in *cooking* endangered species of birds and animals. His dream was to cook the rarest species in the world into extinction. Where most chefs liked to cook meat rare, Marcel La Bouche loved to cook rare meat.

He had a secret list of very special customers who would pay incredible amounts of money for his unique

meals made from rare creatures. From time to time, someone from his network of poachers and hunters would send him 'something special' from some faraway place. Then La Bouche would fly, in his own plane, to anywhere in the world, to cook for those very special, very wealthy customers.

Sitting in his office, Marcel thought back to the great times in the past, when he and his old sidekick, Sam Biddle, had hunted deep in some remote jungle, waiting for hours for some unlucky rare animal to appear — Biddle armed with a rifle, and he, the great Marcel La Bouche, armed with a frying pan .... Oh, the memories!

And there had been so many successes — so many rare creatures made even rarer by his great talent as a master chef. Even now, with all his fame, in his beautiful, expensive restaurant, Marcel found himself longing for one last great challenge ... some animal so rare that to cook it meant its very extinction ....

The phone rang.

Marcel woke from his daydream and picked up the receiver.

"Allo? ... Yes ... Biddle! You old dog! I was just thinking about you ... Eh? You've found something? ... Big grey birds. Maybe they're just seagulls? ... Yes, I know you're not a complete idiot, I'm sorry ... You say they are the size of turkeys?'

Marcel frowned and began flicking through a birdwatching book on his desk, the telephone receiver still held to his ear.

'Some kind of goose, perhaps? ... No? ... Bigger, with funny beaks ....'

Marcel began to lick his lips in excitement.

'Biddle, you might have found something new indeed! ... Yes, of course I shall come to see them ... It will

take a day or two to get myself organised, but — What?
... Yes, of course I will make it worth your while ...
Right. Oh, one thing: does anyone in particular own
these birds? ... Really? ... Well, no matter — it has never
stopped us before ... Right. I will contact you soon.'

When the telephone conversation was over, Marcel
La Bouche sat back in his expensive leather chair and
smiled the smile of a truly happy, if slightly insane,
man.

In the crowded dining room of La Grande Bouche,
the customers continued their oohing and aahing. Of
course, they were totally unaware that Marcel would
soon be taking a holiday — bringing his frying pan
with him.

Chapter Six

The following Saturday, Alex took the bus into Narrowview and visited the small village library. No stranger to the place, he made his way directly to a set of small dark wooden drawers, which held thousands of filing cards arranged in alphabetical order — details of all the books sitting on the dusty shelves around him.

He and Terry had spent the past few evenings with the Professor, being shown around the Miller place. They had walked through the walnut groves, and the Professor had explained how the nuts from all those trees were stored as a food supply for the dodos. They had visited the barns and seen where the birds took shelter from the cold. They had been shown and told so much — and Alex, being Alex, wanted to know so much more. His mind craved facts, graphs, charts ... statistics!

He checked through the yellowing cards in the catalogue files and found what he wanted.

Extinct and Endangered Species of Birds, by J. Daw.

'Yes! Yes! Yes!' he whispered excitedly to himself. Pushing the drawer shut, he approached the librarian with his request.

'Well, well, well!' exclaimed the librarian. 'That book has never, to my knowledge, been taken out before — and now it's requested twice in one day!

Well, well, well!' She shook her head in disbelief at the wonder of it all.

Alex pursed his lips.

'I'm sorry, but you're too late, young man,' the librarian continued. 'A foreign gentleman beat you to it.' Her eyes stared off into space and she said, half to herself, 'French, I think .... He was really quite — quite charming ....'

Then she blushed, her eyes came back into focus and she said, rather briskly, 'Still, never mind. We have lots of far more interesting books in the children's section!'

Alex sighed.

'No, thank you,' he told her, and he left the library to catch the bus home.

The kitchen of Sam Biddle's house was, on the whole, a fairly gloomy sort of place. It doubled as a chicken slaughterhouse; it was here that Biddle Day came to an exciting and sudden end for many of the Pattersons' hens. The odd red splatter on the ceiling or on the damp grey walls bore witness to that.

Sam Biddle was not one for major interior decorating. A grimy cooker and an even grimier sink stood by one wall. In one corner was a rusting fridge, a temporary resting place for some of Mildred 7's less fortunate friends. The floor of once-colourful lino was now a greasy black, with the occasional feather trodden into it. A single bare light-bulb cast a comfortless glare over a rickety table.

The stark light threw two burly shadows on the wall. One was Sam Biddle's; the other belonged to Marcel La Bouche. The two of them were poring over a

large book about extinct and endangered birds which
lay open on the table.

'Come on, come on!' shouted Terry, when Alex finally
arrived back in the farmyard. She was hopping about
in two different-coloured boots, itching to get going. This
evening promised to be special. The Professor thought
that the egg, the last dodo egg, was about to hatch.

'We'll miss the hatching!' she shouted.

'Keep your voice down,' warned Alex. 'I'm coming.'

They set off across the fields to the Miller place, with
Rags running around their feet, tripping them up. They
climbed, once again, through the hole in the wall.
Going in by the front gate was quicker, and they had
been given a key, but Alex and Terry had both agreed
that that would only arouse suspicions.

The Professor was waiting for them in the orchard.
A smile lit up his face when they arrived.

'You've timed it well,' he beamed. 'The egg should
hatch very soon.'

'How's Mildred 7 getting on?' Terry asked as they
walked towards the house.

'Very well,' replied the old man. 'In fact, she has
made a friend of one of the dodos.' He smiled at some
private joke. 'A hen dodo who is named Dotty — you'll
see why when you meet her. Actually, it's her egg that
we're about to see hatching. Now, follow me.'

'Professor, what is the incubation time for a dodo
egg?' enquired Alex as they followed the old man into the
house. He was determined to find out all the details he
could. Having missed that library book still bothered him.

'Twenty-three days, give or take twelve hours, from

laying to hatching,' answered the Professor. 'Here we are!'

They had walked through the kitchen and down some steep steps into the cellar of the old house. They were facing a heavy metal door which looked like the entrance to a bank vault.

The Professor pressed down a large handle, and the door slowly swung open on well-oiled hinges. The twins eagerly peered inside.

'It looks like the inside of a sardine tin,' said Terry.

'The walls, ceiling and floor are all made of stainless steel for hygienic reasons,' explained the Professor. 'And now, I must ask you both to put on these coats, gloves and face-masks.'

'You're certain they are not herons?' demanded Marcel La Bouche for the eleventh time.

'Look, I know what a heron is!' spluttered a flustered and red-faced Sam Biddle. 'Give me some credit.'

They pored over *Extinct and Endangered Species of Birds* by John Daw once again.

'Flamingos?'

'I'm not colour-blind!'

'Yes, but your eyesight is perhaps ....'

Biddle peered angrily at Marcel La Bouche through his thick lenses.

'Yes?' he lisped furiously. 'My eyesight is *what*?'

'Oh, nothing.'

'Hmph .... Let's keep looking. It has to be in here somewhere.'

The two heads once more hovered over the regrettably large book on extinct and endangered birds.

The air-conditioned incubation chamber was filled with tension as the old man and the twins studied the large dodo egg.

'Are you sure it's ready?' whispered Terry.

'It should be,' answered the Professor. 'It's been moving gently for the past couple of days. That's always a sure sign.'

At that moment, the egg gently rolled a little to one side on its bed of cotton wool.

'A lesser spotted egret?' enquired Marcel La Bouche.

'Nah — too thin and spindly — no spots on what I saw,' muttered Sam Biddle.

'A pity,' sighed Marcel. 'I have a list of customers — you know, the special customers — who would pay perhaps a thousand dollars a plate for that.'

'A thousand dollars for a plateful? I'll bet it just tastes like chicken,' taunted Sam Biddle.

'Very expensive chicken!' snapped the world's most famous chef crossly. 'Anyway,' he sniffed, 'whatever I cook always tastes *magnifique*!'

He paused.

'They weren't young ostriches, were they?'

'Let's see a picture of it.'

Moments later, a tiny crack appeared on the egg's surface. In the still, electric, breath-held silence of the chamber, the tiny sounds of fragmenting eggshell could be heard clearly. The crack slowly grew.

'Why not let the parents sit on the egg?' whispered Alex.

'Dodos are usually good parents, but not always. Those eggs in the glass cases upstairs are the result of the parent birds failing to mind their eggs properly. Remember, the climate here is a lot colder than it is in Mauritius,' answered the Professor. 'And at this stage, I couldn't take the risk of even one egg failing.'

Just then, they heard two sets of clawed feet coming down the steps to the cellar. A dodo and a chicken wandered into the chamber.

'Ah! Dotty and Mildred 7,' beamed Professor Miller. 'Well, I suppose it's only fair that you should be here. The egg is hers,' he reminded the twins.

Dotty ambled over to the humans with her new friend. She seemed less interested in her egg than in what the people were wearing on their feet. She gave the Professor's booted feet only a passing glance. She also quickly lost interest in Terry's wellington boots. Alex, however, had finely polished shoes on.

The egg began to rock back and forth. Everybody instantly lost interest in Dotty and returned their attention to the egg.

Dotty gently tugged at one of Alex's shoelaces.

'Wait! That looks a bit like it!' exclaimed an excited Sam Biddle.

'An African Shoebill,' read Marcel. 'Hmm. I haven't cooked one of those before .... And you say you saw about thirty of these?' He fingered the page of the bird book.

'Well, not exactly like these,' explained Biddle. 'The beak is wrong. What I saw was about the same size and shape as this, but the beak looked sharper — sort of like a bottle-opener.'

'Are you sure you didn't open a few bottles yourself?' snorted Marcel. 'Perhaps after a few nips of whiskey your eyesight is not so good, eh? Maybe all you saw was a few turkeys, no?' Marcel's voice was rising.

Sam Biddle's face flushed a deeper shade of red.

'Look,' he roared, 'I saw what I saw! Those birds were strange. It's not my fault they're not in this stupid book!'

With that, he picked up *Extinct and Endangered Species of Birds* by J. Daw and threw it on the floor in disgust.

The pages fluttered and the book opened at the section dealing with extinct species. Biddle glanced down; then he paused; then he tilted his head to get a better view of the large, full-page picture on page twenty-eight.

'Um — Marcel ....' His eyes gleamed. 'Well — um — That's it,' he declared in triumph.

Marcel La Bouche's elegant head snapped in the direction of the open book on the greasy floor. His eyes focused on the picture, then widened in amazement.

'What? This? THIS? ... Are you sure?'

Biddle nodded.

'Certain?'

Biddle nodded again.

'But these have been extinct for centuries! Do you know what this means?'

Biddle shrugged.

'Ten thousand dollars a plate — maybe fifty thousand! I'll be rich!'

Biddle frowned.

'I mean, *we*'ll be rich. Our fortunes are made, and you — you are a genius, Biddle!' Marcel grasped his companion by the shoulders and smacked a kiss on his forehead.

'Hey! Enough of that!' spluttered Sam Biddle gruffly. He peered at the open book on the floor. His lips moved as he tried to read the blurry heading at the top of the page. His eyes weren't up to the task.

'What is it, anyway?' he lisped.

Marcel turned towards him, his eyes glazed over in triumph and delight. He almost whispered in his excitement.

'It's a dodo!'

'It's a dodo!' breathed Alex in wonder, as the newly-hatched chick took its first halting steps from the shell fragments. Unlike Terry, he was still having trouble accepting the fact that these were living, breathing birds. It was hard for Alex to reject any fact which had been printed in a book.

Terry caught the Professor's eye. He smiled and nodded. Gently, carefully, slowly, she put her hands around the chick's downy grey body and picked it up from the incubating table. It did not struggle; it seemed to sense that Terry was no threat. She lightly stroked the chick's downy back. Then, just as carefully as she had picked it up, she put the chick back on the table, where the Professor had placed a small bowl of food for it.

The old man smiled to himself. The girl was a natural: she had handled that precious dodo chick as well as he himself could have.

Alex was interested in seeing the chick have its first meal. He took a step forward — and fell over.

As he picked himself up, he caught the smile on Professor Miller's face.

'I suppose I should have warned you,' the Professor admitted.

Terry pointed to Alex's feet and laughed. His usually perfectly-tied shoelaces were a hopeless mess. Dotty gazed at him innocently.

'She did that?' Alex gasped, gesturing towards the dodo.

'Yes, she does it every chance she gets,' laughed the Professor, as he gently picked up the dodo chick to examine it. 'I've no idea how she learned something as complicated as tying shoelaces together. It's become her party trick. I've given up wearing shoes with laces.'

He pointed to his booted feet.

'Your laced-up shoes must have made her day.'

Dotty, satisfied at having shown off her unusual skills, wandered back up the cellar steps with her new pal, Mildred 7.

Sam Biddle scratched his stubbly chin in sheer wonder.

'And to think,' he said, 'everyone thought they were extinct.'

Marcel laughed.

'And so they will be, my friend! I think I'd better go and have a closer look at them.'

Chapter Seven

Marcel La Bouche — being, at least in his own estimation, a man of great charm and superior intelligence — approached the task of stealing the dodos with great subtlety.

Biddle — being a more crude individual, who tended to act first and think later — had suggested that they break into the Miller place, tie up the Professor, round up the dodos, and make a quick getaway.

'No!' Marcel decided firmly. 'No, no, no! Leave it to me, Biddle. I shall thoroughly research the whole business and then come up with a marvellous plan worthy of a La Bouche!'

Biddle grunted and sidled off, muttering to himself about damn fool Frenchmen and making simple tasks complicated.

Marcel La Bouche's research started at the Hooray Henery Chicken Farm.

Mrs Patterson was putting the final touches to a twelve-egg omelette for the family dinner when the long, shining, jet-black Citroën car slid regally into the yard. She watched through the window as the tall Frenchman climbed out of his car and looked slowly all around.

'I know that nose,' she gasped excitedly. 'I know that nose!'

The omelette was beginning to burn, but Mrs Patterson was distracted by the approaching stranger.

'It's that chef fellow!' she exclaimed. 'The fellow from the telly!'

She quivered all over with excitement. Leaving the smoking omelette, she rushed to the door, hastily wiping egg yolk off her fingers onto her dress.

'I know you,' she cried as she pulled open the door. 'You are Marcel the Marvellous, from the telly, aren't you? I never miss your cookery programme. I'd know your nose anywhere. It's so — so — so *big*!' she finished, all a-wobble with glee.

'I am charmed, Madame,' purred Marcel La Bouche, bestowing his most winning smile on the woman; and, bending down to her (for Mrs Patterson was rather short and very fat), he kissed her on both cheeks — cheeks which immediately began to redden.

'Oh my,' she giggled, 'kissed by Marcel the Marvellous. This is the greatest day of my life!'

Marcel beamed down at her.

'Madame — would something, perhaps, be burning?' he enquired politely. And indeed, black smoke was billowing out of the kitchen.

'Oh my!' cried Mrs Patterson, rushing back into the kitchen. She grabbed the burnt pan and flung the blackened remains of the twelve-egg omelette out of the window, into the yard, where a delighted Rags grabbed it and ran off.

'What must you think?' Mrs Patterson asked the famous chef, her face flushed with embarrassment. 'And you such a great cook from the telly!'

'Madame, think nothing of it — it could happen even to a bishop. I am here because your wonderful egg creations are the talk of the town.'

'Are they?' asked Mrs Patterson, completely taken aback.

'I want to know *everything*,' simpered Marcel. 'How do *you*, Madame — how do *you* boil an egg?'

'Well,' began Mrs Patterson, 'first I —'

'You must appear on my programme. I shall do a Scrambled Egg Special in the spring. You shall be the star!'

'Me?' exclaimed the twins' incredulous mother, puffing herself up. 'Me, a star?'

'Yes, yes, yes,' interrupted Marcel. 'But first, tell me something about this neighbour of yours. He is a chicken farmer too, is he not?'

'Miller? I don't know much about him,' stammered Mrs Patterson. 'He only appears in the village once a month or so.'

'On what day exactly? At what hour exactly, woman?' snapped Marcel, his patience with this silly woman wearing a bit thin.

'On the first Tuesday of every month, from three to four,' said a man's voice.

Marcel spun around. Mr Patterson's oil-splattered face looked in at him from the doorway.

'Is the tractor fixed, love?' asked Mrs Patterson, also quite surprised to see her husband there.

'No, but I was hungry and I smelled omelette,' Mr Patterson explained. He held out his hand to Marcel La Bouche.

'Patterson's the name,' he said, 'and poultry farming is the game.'

'Yes, yes, that's right,' mumbled Marcel. Barely touching Patterson's greasy hand, he edged past him, out the door and into the yard. 'And now I must depart.'

'But Marcel,' called Mrs Patterson, 'you said that —'

'I will be in touch, Madame,' called the retreating
chef. Blowing Mrs Patterson a kiss, he climbed quickly
into his car and sped away.

'Weird!' muttered Mr Patterson, shaking his head.
'Seriously weird.'

But Marcel La Bouche, the intrepid investigator, had
found out what he wanted to know. 'Tuesday from
three to four,' he told himself, hitting the accelerator
and racing through the puddles of the Pattersons'
driveway. 'That is when we will strike!' he declared,
and nearly drove into a ditch as he swerved to avoid
two horrible children on their way home from school.

Marcel stopped the car. 'You should be pan-fried,
you crazy lunatics!' he roared at them through his open
window.

'And you should be jailed, Mister!' roared Terry,
who had fallen on her backside in a puddle.

La Bouche looked from Terry to Alex. The boy was
staring into the back of the car. Marcel swung around
sharply to see what he was looking at so intently.

On the back seat lay the tome *Extinct and Endangered
Species* by John Daw.

Marcel looked at Alex. Their eyes locked for an in-
stant. The boy seemed to look straight into La Bouche's
head.

Marcel slammed in the clutch and roared off down
the lane.

Chapter Eight

The doors of La Grande Bouche Restaurant were locked, and the chairs were stacked on the tabletops. But for the two figures huddled over one table in a dimly-lit corner of the room, the restaurant was empty.

'Well?' asked Sam Biddle, noisily sucking a long string of spaghetti into his mouth. 'What's the great La Bouche plan?'

Marcel La Bouche looked at his companion in disgust. Sauce was dripping down Biddle's chin and falling in great red blobs onto his shirt (Marcel had insisted that Biddle wear some decent clothes when he visited him in his smart city restaurant). The shirt, and most of the jacket of his ill-fitting suit, was now a sticky mess. Food slopped about his mouth as he spoke — it was like watching a cement mixer in action. Bits of spaghetti lay on the carpeted floor like some kind of worm massacre.

Marcel shuddered. Thank goodness Biddle had come in through the back door.

'Watching you eat makes me feel like throwing up,' complained La Bouche.

'Ha! You fussy foreigner!' laughed Sam Biddle, not in the least embarrassed, food spraying out of his mouth as he spoke. A few high-flying bits of half-chewed spaghetti managed to land on Marcel's crisp white shirt. La Bouche pursed his lips and fought down

the urge to tip Biddle's plate of food onto his lap. He
still needed Biddle in order to carry out his plan. So,
instead, he closed his eyes and proceeded to explain his
brilliant idea.

'This is the La Bouche plan: on Tuesday next, at 3.15
p.m. precisely, we two shall break into the Miller place,
round up the dodos and make a quick getaway.'

'Great plan! Marvellous!' sneered Sam Biddle with a
laugh. 'I'd never have thought of that!'

'Indeed,' agreed La Bouche, quite seriously. 'Its
beauty is in its simplicity and directness, is it not? It is a
plan worthy of the great Napoleon himself!'

'And what if the Professor comes back too soon?'
enquired Biddle, slurping up another long strand of
spaghetti through sauce-smeared lips.

'Then we will have to slit his throat,' replied Marcel
La Bouche, in the same tone of voice that a sane person
would use to read out a shopping list.

'Right!' laughed Sam Biddle. 'I'll bet your friend
Napoleon would approve of that too!' He was in good
form, very proud of his part in discovering the dodos,
and looking forward to his share of the money they
would make. Even the meal — though not quite as
good as his favourite, chicken livers and chips —
wasn't bad; and Sam Biddle was a man who enjoyed
his food. He was also a man who enjoyed slitting
throats.

He wiped some of the sauce off his chin with the
back of his hand. Marcel La Bouche winced.

'When do we head back to Narrowview?' Sam Biddle
asked, as the last little blob of sauce dripped from his
chin.

'The sooner the better,' replied Marcel. 'I have all of
the equipment ready — even ... the Machine.'

'The Machine!' Biddle sat bolt upright. 'You're not going to use — the Machine ... are you?' He gulped.

'But of course!' snapped Marcel. 'We need to work fast. I want those birds killed and in pieces as quickly as possible.'

'Yes,' stammered Sam Biddle, 'but ... the Machine ....' He went pale. 'You remember what happened the last time?'

'Look,' said Marcel, 'those men should have been more careful.' He studied his fingernails. 'Anyway, their bodies were never found.'

'There wasn't much left to find,' mumbled Sam Biddle under his breath.

'What? ... Oh, very witty! It's all ready. There's an old airfield near the place. I will have everything set up in an old aircraft hangar there. My plane will be fully ready and waiting to get us and our — ah — *ingredients* away safely.'

'You're using the plane as well?' Biddle was impressed.

'Listen, my friend. If those birds really are what you say they are, then it will all be worth it,' purred Marcel. 'We will do it next Tuesday. With luck, the old man will be away long enough for everything to go smoothly.'

Chapter Nine

A shining blue van and a stylish French car pulled up outside the gates of Professor Miller's place. The car was towing a large, covered trailer.

A figure emerged from each vehicle.

'Eh, Biddle, this is no time for you to polish your van!'

'Just a spot ... Eh? ... Oh! Right, let's go!'

They stood at the foot of the high wall and looked up. Then they began.

It was like watching a stick insect and a beetle trying to climb a shoebox, neither of them doing very well. The two intrepid climbers were soon sitting, red-faced and sweating, at the bottom of the wall — on the same side where they had begun.

'It's no good,' gasped Sam Biddle. 'We'll never get in!'

'Nonsense!' snapped Marcel La Bouche. 'Give me — how you say — a leg up. Now!'

Grumbling, Sam Biddle bent down and cupped his hands together. Marcel stepped onto Biddle's hands and then up onto his shoulders. Biddle gasped and staggered under the weight.

'Hold still, you idiot!' ordered the world's most famous insane chef. 'I can reach the top of the wall.'

One foot stepped onto Sam Biddle's head. 'Got it!' The second foot tried to gain a hold on top of the head. They were big feet. Sam Biddle's head was small.

Still, an ear would do.

'Aaaargh!'

'Quiet, you fool! Someone perhaps will hear us!'

'Hmmmph ... eeeeeh ... aaaaagh!'

'Oh, stop whimpering. I'm nearly there.' A heel dug into the back of Biddle's skull.

It was then that the soft ground beneath Sam Biddle began to give way. Slowly, his feet started to slide away from the wall. He clutched desperately at the rough wall; his fingernails scrabbled at the stone, but one by one they broke and lost their hold.

It was quite painful.

'Yeeeooooowww!'

'What is it now? Stop moving! I'm nearly up. What are you doing?'

'It's my feet,' whimpered the agonised Sam Biddle. 'They're slipping in the mud.'

'Well, do something, you idiot!' snapped Marcel La Bouche. With that, he deftly kicked the back of Biddle's head with his 'ear' foot. The momentary relief to Sam Biddle's ear was more than cancelled out by the fact that his face had been brought into painful contact with the wall. The left lens of his thick glasses was cracked like a cobweb.

However, he had indeed stopped sliding in the mud. He hadn't realised you could hold onto a wall with your nose. It had begun to bleed.

'There, I have placed the rug over the broken glass. I climb up now.'

Suddenly all of La Bouche's weight was removed from Sam Biddle's head. He felt as though someone had switched off gravity — not that it did him much good: he lost his nasal grip on the wall, slid, and slumped onto the muddy ground.

Marcel, of course, was full of encouragement.

'This is no time to rest! Get up, you oaf! I will see if I can open the gates from the inside.'

Professor Aidan Miller was having a successful day in the village. For once, there hadn't been a gigantic queue in the post office, and he had got his business

sorted out quickly. A very important letter had just
been sent to his lawyers. He smiled as he thought of the
twins. After all, they were about the nearest he had to
family.

The other errands had soon been sorted out, too. It
would be good to get back home early.

The blue van and the French car had been hidden
beneath some trees just off the driveway. The gates had
been shut again. Marcel La Bouche and Sam Biddle,
walking up the driveway, came to a leaf-covered patch
in the lane; the old man obviously didn't have a car.
Biddle hurried ahead a little, eager to prove to Marcel
that he had been right about the birds. Suddenly, he
disappeared through the leaves.

It was only a two-metre fall, but in Biddle's already
painful state, it came as a nasty shock. He lay face
down in the hole, moaning softly to himself.

'Eh, Biddle, no time to play around! Lucky for me
you find this trap first, yes? Get up, quick!'

As soon as Sam Biddle hauled himself out of the
hole (it was a dog trap, actually), he realised that the
right lens of his glasses had fallen out and been lost. He
sighed. He wondered if, when he was rich, he would
be able to afford nice thick contact lenses. The thought
cheered him up, a little.

'Let us stay off the lane,' suggested Marcel. 'There
might be more like that. You go first, to — ah — show
the way, yes?'

Professor Miller enjoyed the stroll home. It had been a pleasant day, and he was looking forward to the late afternoon, when the twins would come over to visit. Terry really had an amazing way with the dodos — they followed her as readily as they would him — and Alex had come up with some very clever ideas about how to organise the work better. Perhaps someday they would carry on the Miller family's work. They certainly had the ability. It was just as well that he had written to his lawyers.

He turned into the narrow country road which led to his own house and to the Pattersons' farm.

Sam Biddle looked like a sad, overstuffed owl as he dangled upside down in the net among the walnut trees. He was a good deal heavier than the twins, and the net hung near to the ground, bending the branch to which it was tied. Biddle's head kept knocking the ground with a dull, hollow thump as the branch rose and fell with his weight. He was getting a terrible headache.

'Your brains, they are puréed, Biddle! Why can you not watch where you are going? I don't know what you would do if I were not here to save you from your foolish predicaments. Now push yourself together!'

The cut net and its battered cargo fell to the ground. Easing himself up gingerly, Sam Biddle followed Marcel towards the barns. He reached his boss just as La Bouche was about to open the door of the first barn.

It swung open on rusted hinges. The two men stared at what they saw inside.

The Professor stopped to look into the pit in the drive-way. The covering of leaves was scattered, but the pit was empty ... hmm, perhaps a cat. Best check in on the dodos.

He hadn't noticed the large car, or the trailer, or the blue van hidden beneath the trees. The cut nets of the dog trap lay, out of sight, beneath a bush.

He left his bag of shopping by the front door of the house and went around to the dodo barns. He stopped to check the levels in the walnut storage boxes in one of the outhouses. The dodos loved walnuts. It was just as well his entire garden was planted with dozens of huge walnut trees.

What was that? A grating, creaking sound! Professor Miller turned to listen .... Nothing. He smiled — must be getting dotty in his old age!

He closed the wooden door of the walnut shed — There it was! A rustling noise!

Better check this out ....

Walking as quietly as his boots would allow, the Professor left the shed and moved, following the wall, towards the corner of the building. Something wasn't right. He could feel it.

A rustle. He froze. Something was around the cor-ner. Not a cat, not a dog or a rat; he knew their sounds, had heard them countless times before as he waged his good-natured war against them. This was different.

Professor Miller crouched down, ready to dart around the corner, to confront whatever it was. He could feel his heart pounding. He found himself wish-ing for a good-sized stick. He looked around for something to use, but there was nothing to hand.

Armed with nothing except a little reluctant cour-age, he swung himself low around the corner of the shed — and found himself staring straight into a pair of beady yellow eyes.

The owner of the eyes took one startled step backwards and glared disapprovingly at him.

'Buc-buc-bucaw!'

Mildred 7. The Professor, on his hands and knees, let his body slump with sheer relief and gave a long sigh.

'You old fool!' he muttered to himself, slowly getting to his feet. Of course, he wasn't used to the sound of a hen scratching around in his yard! The Professor allowed himself a moment to get his breath back, then headed towards the dodo barns. He had been so certain that there was something wrong! This annoyed him: he usually had good instincts and good judgement — and then to get flustered and panic over an old hen!

As the Professor neared the first of the dodo barns, Mildred 7 resumed her cautious pecking by the walnut store. That was odd; she usually followed him, eager to see Dotty and the other dodos. Still, he had probably scared her, jumping out on her like that. Nice old chicken, really.

As he lifted the latch on the door of the first barn, Professor Miller thought he glimpsed a movement, out of the corner of his eye. Maybe Mildred had decided to join him after all. The door of the barn swung open and the old man took his first step inside. He didn't get a chance to take a second one.

Hands grabbed him from behind and pushed him roughly against the doorjamb. He struck his forehead against the hard surface. His heart pounded with fear. The sharp pang of adrenaline in his blood gripped painfully at his lower back. He had never felt terror like this before. Part of him refused to believe it was even happening. But he could feel the trickle of blood running down the side of his face, and he knew that this whole sudden, shocking nightmare was all too real.

'What do you want?' he stammered. 'I have money in the house. I'll get it for you.'

'No, no, my friend,' a smug voice gloated in his ear. 'We want something a lot more unusual than money.'

The Professor's legs buckled with shock and he sagged to the ground. They knew!

A sharp, cold steel blade pressed into his throat.

'You surprised us by coming back so early,' the oily, smirking voice continued. 'And yet, it is just as well that you did. Your birds are awkward to control. You will help us to load them into our trailer.'

'And what if I refuse?' The Professor was becoming more angry than frightened.

Rough hands spun him around. He found himself staring at his two captors. One of them had broken glasses and a cut face; he held the knife to the Professor's throat and leered.

'You'd better not refuse,' he lisped. His face was livid. He really seemed to be enjoying himself. 'You'd better not,' he repeated, for want of something else to say.

'Now, now,' the taller man crooned in soothing tones, 'there is no need to be like this. I am sure that you really want to help us. Or ...' — he paused dramatically — 'perhaps you would like us all to wait for your two little children friends to come and help us instead?'

The Professor was trapped, and he knew it. He couldn't allow the twins to fall into the hands of those two thugs. Defeated, he nodded quietly and sighed.

Within minutes, a large car had towed a covered trailer to the yard where the barns were. It took only a few more minutes for Dotty and all the other dodos to placidly follow the Professor to the trailer. They were so trusting, he thought in despair ....

Soon all fifty-four birds were huddled in the roomy trailer. The tailgate was closed.

The fat thug with the broken glasses pointed. 'I see a chicken!' It was Mildred 7.

'Oh, leave it!' snapped the thin one. He turned to the Professor. 'Thank you so much,' he smirked.

'What are you going to do with them?' asked the Professor. 'Do you run some kind of private zoo?'

There was a note of hope in his voice. A zoo would at least mean survival for the dodos.

The tall stranger laughed. His face was ugly with triumph.

'Oh no, my friend,' he purred, in almost-sympathetic tones. 'I run ... a restaurant.'

He laughed again and got into the car. He called to the fat man.

'Finish up here. Then follow me to the airfield. You know what to do?'

Sam Biddle pushed the horrified Professor towards the house.

'I know what to do, all right,' he jeered.

Chapter Ten

Ever since Marcel the Marvellous had visited Mrs Patterson, the twins' mother had been on Cloud Nine. Every egg that the children collected was used for her cooking creations. She was going to be on television! Her moment was at hand and she was going to astound the world! She would soon be a household name!

Not all of her great works were appreciated by her ungrateful children — but is a prophetess ever recognised in her own land? Her occasional unsuccessful attempts were appreciated by Rags. The dog had taken up more or less permanent residence outside the kitchen window. There he would wait patiently, head on paws, for the telltale black smoke to waft out the window. He would hear Mrs Patterson's throaty singing (usually country and western) change to cursing. He would cock his ear when the bashing of pots and pans began; and finally he would gaze in satisfaction as her latest failure came sailing out the window to his waiting jaws.

Rags had fared well since Marcel's visit — and it was still only Tuesday. To date he had sampled and enjoyed burnt Egg and Jelly à la Crème, burnt Omelette and Custard Crumble, burnt Blackberry, Onion and Egg Pie, burnt Egg-Flavoured Ice Cream, and a host of other mouth-watering egg dishes – all burnt to a cinder. He was indeed a happy and increasingly rotund dog. All his years of chewing at tractor tyres had developed his appetite for rubbery foods.

Only at mealtimes did he move indoors and stealthily creep under the kitchen table to rest his nose on Terry's feet.

Mr Patterson must have had the constitution of a horse. He downed all of his wife's culinary delights with relish. Alex was more discerning, but he was too polite and too considerate of his mother's feelings not to clear his plate, even if it did make his stomach churn and his face turn a pale green.

Terry hated the egg meals that her mother made. Egg and Peach Burgers made her sick. The very sight of Scrambled Egg and Rhubarb sent her running to the bathroom. But Terry was a kind girl, and faced with Mrs Patterson's hopeful enquiry of 'Do you like that, Terry?', what could she say?

'It's wonderful, Mam,' she'd smile in a sickly way. As soon as her mother had turned her back, Terry would deftly tip her plate onto the floor for Rags to finish. If it had not been for Professor Miller feeding her up every evening when the twins visited him, Terry would have fallen ill with starvation.

On Tuesday afternoon, while La Bouche and Biddle were scaling the wall of the Miller place, Mrs Patterson was serving her family a delicious delicacy which she had been working on all morning.

'And today we have, for your delight ... Poached Egg and Sardine Curry followed by delicious Home-made Egg and Peanut Butter Ice Cream!' she announced importantly to her grim-faced children and her smiling husband.

'Sounds good, love,' declared Mr Patterson, licking his lips.

'When exactly are you going to appear on TV?' asked Terry, trying not to look at her plate. Alex had taken a forkful and was swallowing hard.

'Oh, Marcel didn't say exactly when — but any day now, I expect,' replied their mother breezily. 'Such a charming man,' she continued, glad to be on her favourite subject. 'He's had his difficulties, though.'

'What difficulties?' asked Alex, distracting his mother long enough for Terry to feed half her plateful to Rags.

'Well, he's been the subject of vicious rumours. The restaurant business is very competitive, you know,' Mrs Patterson explained.

'I know,' agreed Alex, pushing his food about the plate while Terry off-loaded another pile of hers onto the floor.

'Some of Marcel's envious, jealous, evil competitors spread scurrilous rumours about him. They claimed that he was serving his customers some rare, protected reptile or other in one of his restaurants. The very idea of it!'

'Really?' asked Alex, suddenly sitting up and taking note. Terry shot him a look.

'Lies, of course, all lies,' continued their mother. 'Vicious lies and innuendo — but there was a court case and a great to-do. Of course, Marcel was completely innocent. Such a lovely, polite man — with such a fine Gallic nose!'

'How do you know all this, Mam?' asked Terry, glancing at Alex, her food forgotten.

Mr Patterson was enjoying his food and paid no heed to the conversation.

'Great meal, lovey,' he said happily.

'Nice of you to say so,' replied his wife, beaming with pleasure and forgetting Terry's question.

'Tell us more about Marcel the Marvellous,' said Alex abruptly.

'He has top-class restaurants all over the world. I saw it all on a documentary about him,' explained Mrs

Patterson. 'And do you know that he has his own private plane? He flies all over the world to keep an eye on his restaurants.'

'He's a nasty crook,' muttered Terry, but luckily her mother didn't hear her.

'Did he ask about Professor Miller?' demanded Alex.

'Oh, that old crackpot,' giggled Mrs Patterson. 'I don't know what has you children fascinated with that man.'

'Did he mention him, Mammy?' Terry nearly shrieked.

'As a matter of fact, he did. He wanted to know when Miller went out. Anyway, I think Marcel wants me to star in his autumn series —'

'And you told him, didn't you?' shouted Terry, jumping up from the table and racing out of the room.

'Of course I did. What's got into that girl? And her dinner only half eaten!' the twins' mother demanded indignantly.

'Excuse me, Mother and Father, but I also have to leave — *now*,' announced Alex, pushing his chair back from the table and chasing after Terry.

Rags charged after the children, leaving their mother totally bewildered.

'Well, really!' she declared.

'Never mind, lovey,' said Mr Patterson. 'I'll finish off their dinners. Best meal you've ever made!' And he pulled Alex's plate towards him.

Chapter Eleven

Sam Biddle had been enjoying himself thoroughly. Pushing a frightened, hurt old man around was just his idea of a good time.

He had tied the Professor up in the cellar of the house. The old man was in no state to put up a fight. Marcel had really taken the wind out of his sails with that crack about owning a restaurant! Biddle decided he would finish the old fellow off soon ... but maybe he'd have a little look around first. Perhaps take a few souvenirs. There were bound to be some valuable trinkets around. It'd be a shame to burn them too. Sam Biddle told himself that he had a little time to kill .... Time to kill! He cackled at his own joke.

The house had a few bits and pieces — a watch, a nice little clock .... Biddle decided to go out to the barns to see if there was anything there.

That was when the problems began.

Biddle's glasses were useless. The right lens was gone. The left lens was a shattered mess. So his right eye saw a single blurred image, while his left eye could see at least nineteen tiny distorted ones.

And then the fog began to roll in. The blurry, distorted shapes which he had been able to make out in the house dissolved into a thick, pearly grey mist. He was as good as blind.

Biddle stumbled over, and fell into, a water trough. The fact that he was soaked to the skin and that his shins were very badly scraped hardly put a dent in his cheerful mood. But the second fall, this time over a feed bin, resulted in a painfully sprained thumb; and then, still nursing his injured thumb, Biddle walked straight into a wall. It was hardly fair — the wall was the same colour as the fog. Now he had a really awful headache. A tiny bit of his cheerful mood had evaporated.

With a more characteristic grumble, Biddle turned towards where he thought the house was. The thought of the old man waiting helplessly there for him brought a grim smile to his bruised lips. It took only three more stumbles and two changes of direction before he reached the house.

Just inside the front door stood the petrol can which he had unloaded from the blue van. He'd be needing that petrol soon. It would all have to look like an accident — the old man tripping over in the cellar while a fire was left unattended, something like that .... Anyway, the old house would go up in a flash. There wouldn't be anything left to raise any suspicions.

Biddle had some difficulty opening the lid of the petrol can — his knuckles were stiff after that last fall up the steps to the front door. With a small grunt of triumph, he tossed the lid on the floor and began to spill petrol over the carpet. With luck, he'd have enough to pour over the entire ground floor of the house.

As he passed by the door leading to the cellar, he paused to peer down. The Professor was still tied to a tall wooden chair beside a work table. Sam Biddle's left eye could make out at least nineteen images of the old man's head moving slightly. He was awake. Good!

Biddle wanted him to know exactly what was going to happen to him. He chuckled to himself and carried on with his pouring.

Hold it! There was a sound! Biddle's eyes weren't up to much at the moment, but there was nothing wrong with his hearing. Those two brats must have arrived!

His heart began to beat wildly. He fumbled for his matches. Then he stopped.

Biddle smiled. A truly magnificent idea had just crossed his mind.

Instead of one tragic death in the fire, he might just be able to manage three.

He hurried down the stairs to the cellar. Even with his poor eyesight, he quickly found a dark corner to lurk in. After all, those two little brats would hardly be a match for the great Sam Biddle!

Terry, being the quicker runner, was the first to arrive at the gates of the Miller place. It would have taken too long to go through the fields and use the hole in the wall; the Professor had given them a key to the front gates, and they both felt a terrible need to get to the house as quickly as possible.

Terry stopped dead in her tracks when she saw that the gates were open.

'Alex!' she whispered loudly.

She could hear his running footsteps approaching, but the thick fog meant that she couldn't see him until he was only a few paces away.

'The gates are open. Something's wrong,' she told her brother.

Alex wiped away the beads of moisture which had

formed on his glasses, and got his breath back. Rags cowered at Alex's feet, his tail between his legs.

'It's very quiet, isn't it?' said Alex. He could feel the hair standing up on the back of his neck. His feet made a rustling noise in the wet leaves of the driveway. The sound seemed very loud in the eerie stillness of the fog.

'Take off your boots, Alex,' ordered Terry quietly, pulling off her own. He nodded and followed her example.

'We must proceed with extreme caution,' warned Alex. Terry almost smiled at her brother's precise words — but this was no time for smiling.

They quickly threw their boots under some bushes by the gate. Alex took the lead, walking silently up the driveway in his stocking feet. Terry followed him closely — visibility was almost nil. The fog rested like a grey blanket over the Miller place, hiding its dangers.

Alex walked straight into Sam Biddle's blue van. It seemed to rear up out of the fog at them. Terry, normally the daredevil, clutched Alex's arm. Rags growled.

'It's Biddle's!' whispered Alex. 'What's he doing here?'

'No good — you can be sure of that,' said Terry. 'He's evil. I hate him!'

'I hope the Professor is safe,' said Alex quietly. He was very frightened. Alex was not normally given to irrational fears, but the fog and the blue van and the eerie silence hanging over the whole place terrified him. Terry, with her wild imagination, felt no better. It would be so easy to turn and run back down the driveway .... It took all of their courage not to do exactly that.

The twins glanced at each other.

Terry mouthed, 'Let's check the dodos,' and they crept past the van in the direction of the first barn. Their socks were wet and muddy and the gravel cut into their feet, but the children hardly noticed.

They both knew the layout of the Miller place quite well by now; but the dense fog swirled about them like thick smoke, teasing them, making the walk to the yard seem longer than it ever had before — and more treacherous. Once-familiar objects loomed out of the mist like living things — a water trough, an old tractor tyre ....

Suddenly, a great shadowy figure spread out huge arms over their heads. They both let out a cry and gripped each other in terror. But it was just a walnut tree, appearing out of the fog.

'Do you think we're being followed?' whispered Terry.

'The fog hides us as well as them,' answered Alex, in as sensible-sounding a voice as he could manage.

At last they found the first barn. The door was shut, but its heavy bolt was pulled back.

The twins looked quickly at each other. The thought crossed both of their minds that somebody could be inside.

Terry nodded once to Alex. He swallowed and pulled the door open. It creaked in the silence.

Sam Biddle stood stock-still. They were checking the barns — that was the creak. Soon they would discover that the dodos were gone, and then they would come looking for the Professor.

Biddle grinned to himself. From his hiding-place he

could see the old man tied to the chair, the gag cutting into his cheeks, his eyes darting wildly about. He had heard the creaking door as well.

Biddle calculated. He'd have to wait for maybe five minutes, ten at the most. He squinted his eyes and tried to focus on the stairs that the children would have to come down.

Terry bit her bottom lip. Tears of anger were welling up in her eyes. The dodos were gone! All the Professor's work, the years of trying and hoping — all wasted, all gone. She didn't feel frightened any more; she just felt angry. Biddle and that other creep, La Bouche! Terry was fit to explode.

Alex could see the signs, so he put a finger to his lips in warning. Terry said nothing.

'Let's try the house,' Alex whispered. 'We've got to find the Professor.'

Terry sniffed, wiped her nose quickly on her sleeve, and nodded.

Keeping their backs to the wall of the barn, the twins crept towards the house. Rags was crawling on his belly, his ears flat against his head and his teeth bared.

The fog began to lift slightly and the house emerged, large and black and ghostly. The back door was open. Taking a deep breath to steady themselves, the twins went in.

The kitchen was dark; there was no light on. As soon as Terry and Alex were in the room, a terrible smell of petrol hit their noses. They moved slowly across the cold flagstones of the kitchen floor; the old table and chairs stood like silent witnesses to whatever had happened — and whatever would happen next.

On the other side of the kitchen was a door leading to the back hallway. Through that doorway, a patch of light came from the cellar stairs.

'I'm going down,' whispered Alex.

'So am I,' hissed Terry.

Rags stopped and sat, whining quietly, in the doorway which led back to the kitchen. He lay down, his head on his paws, and watched the twins go down the cellar steps and out of sight.

The cellar light was very bright after the gloom of the fog, and both of the children felt exposed and vulnerable as they slowly descended the last few steps. The light dazzled them.

Sarn Biddle was well hidden. He had moved into the shadows beneath the stairs when he heard the twins in the hallway above. Through the cobweb cracks of what was left of his glasses, he could see a confused jumble of stocking feet pass within an arm's length of his head as the children came down the stairs. He heard them gasp and cry out when they saw the Professor roped to the chair. And then, just as Sam Biddle had known they would, the twins rushed across the cellar to the old man.

Time to move! Biddle slipped out of the shadows and groped his way towards the foot of the stairs.

He imagined the Professor's eyes wildly darting this way and that as he tried to warn the little brats. Too late! They had reached the old man and were tugging at his ropes, as Biddle had known they would. They were so predictable!

Biddle went up the stairs backwards, spilling petrol as he climbed. Of course, the children didn't hear him — he had taken off his shoes too. Anyway, they were too busy firing questions at the Professor; but he couldn't answer, because they couldn't get the gag off him. The twins' backs were to the stairs, but the Professor could see everything, and his eyes were wide with horror.

Terry tore at the gag.

'We thought you were dead!' she shouted.

'He will be!' called Sam Biddle, from the top of the stairs. He laughed loudly as the twins swung around, just in time to see him spill the last of the petrol down the steps.

'And so will you!' he cackled, scraping a match along the sandpapered edge of the matchbox.

Chapter Twelve

Rags cowered a few paces from the top of the cellar stairs. He could hear the twins' voices, and he could hear the fear in the way they spoke. His ears could tell him all this, but his nose was useless to him: the terrible smell of petrol blocked out all other smells. He could not smell friend from foe. A soft whine came from his throat.

Suddenly his ears picked up a new sound — a voice. It sounded cruel, dangerous — and yet familiar.

'He will be!'

Something large emerged from the cellar doorway. Something large and round.

'And so will you!' An ugly laugh. The large, round thing loomed out of the doorway towards Rags.

There was a scrapy, scratchy noise. More ugly laughing. Rags could hear the twins sounding very frightened.

Biddle!

The chicken man! Biddle the kicker! Biddle, Rags's tormentor!

Somewhere, deep within the small dog, the dam wall of a huge reservoir of hatred broke open. His great enemy, his mortal enemy, had presented him with the target of his dreams.

All right, so Rags was a cross between a collie and a chihuahua. But long ago — maybe hundreds of years, maybe thousands — his ancestors had been wolves. And the fear in his friends' voices and the sight of his tormentor's great round backside brought out the wolf in Rags.

His teeth were bared; his hind legs tensed like coiled springs; a last moment of poise — and then he leaped. Front paws extended, muscles rippling, he flew, a furry, ferocious fury, towards his target. In what seemed an eternity but was, in fact, less than a second, Rags's sharp little teeth had made powerful, deep and immensely satisfying contact with Sam Biddle's bottom.

Biddle had been too busy chuckling and trying to strike the matches (they were still a little soggy from his fall in the water trough) to notice the tiny sounds and movements behind him. His fingers were still fairly sore, and it was hard to focus, through one shattered lens, on what looked like nineteen matchboxes.

Still, there was absolutely no way those brats could get away this time. They'd go up in a flash, and he'd be out the back door of the house in seconds flat.

He did hear a snarl, but it all happened so quickly that he had no time even to turn around. He heard the crunch as the dog's teeth bit firmly into what was, after all, just about the only part of his body which wasn't cut or bruised. And there was another thing —

He was falling ...

down the cellar stairs ...

at quite a respectable speed ...

quite painfully ...

smacking his chin off the steps as he went ...

with a dog attached to his bottom ...

and there was the cellar floor ....

Darkness.

Rags, triumphant, finally let go his grip on Sam Biddle and stood, the clear winner, on the upturned backside of his moaning, defeated enemy. It was his finest moment.

Alex and Terry wasted no time. With trembling hands, they finally freed the Professor.

'We must hurry,' he gasped. 'An evil madman has captured the dodos!'

A look of horror spread across his face.

'He wants to cook them!'

As they helped him to his feet, the old man told the twins about the trailer-load of dodos heading for the airfield.

'We'd better call the police,' said Alex.

'Will they get here in time?' asked Terry, running up the stairs. There was a phone in the kitchen.

By the time Alex and Professor Miller got to the bottom of the stairs, she was calling down to them.

'The phone's wrecked! They thought of everything.'

'It's hopeless,' mumbled the Professor. 'All those years of hope and work ... wasted!'

A moan came from Sam Biddle, still lying on the cellar floor. Rags growled.

'Perhaps not,' said Alex suddenly. 'Terry, come down here. We need to make sure that Mr Biddle won't trouble us.'

Alex searched Sam Biddle's pockets. He handed the Professor back his old watch. From another of Biddle's pockets came a beautiful little clock ... some money ... and then, bingo! A set of keys. The keys to the blue van.

Alex held up the keys for the other two to see.

'We haven't lost yet!' he grinned.

'Right,' said Terry, 'what'll we do with old Biddle here?'

All three heads turned, as one, towards the incubation chamber which stood in a corner of the cellar.

'Yes, that should hold him,' said Terry, grinning.

The Professor was still fairly shaken after his ordeal, so the twins each grabbed a leg and dragged Sam Biddle across the cellar floor. Rags followed, growling, ready for any trouble. There was none. The fight had definitely gone out of Sam Biddle for the time being.

'That should cool him off!' declared Alex.

Well, perhaps not. But the twins weren't to know that as they jammed the chair against the door of the incubation chamber, they had accidentally raised its temperature-control setting to 'VERY HOT'.

They helped the Professor up the stairs and out into the misty night air.

'I only hope we're not too late,' the Professor said anxiously, as the three of them made their way through the fog to Sam Biddle's blue van.

The twins retrieved their boots from the bushes and put them on. The Professor leaned against a gatepost, holding a handkerchief to his forehead and mopping the blood from a cut.

'I'll be all right in a minute,' he tried to assure them.

Terry looked at Alex, and then at the blue van.

'It's up to us, isn't it?' she said.

Her brother nodded. He looked at the blue van again. Drops of water from the fog sat like glass beads on its beautifully polished paintwork.

Alex blinked. This was no time for careful thought or exact logic. They had to move fast.

'Terry, help the Professor into the van,' he ordered. 'I'm driving.'

He unlocked the passenger door and went around to the driver's side. The passenger seat was wide enough that both Terry and the old man could sit in it. Rags had shot past them and piled himself into the back of the van. Alex climbed into the driver's seat.

'Right,' he said, pulling the seat as far forward as it would go. 'Where do you put the key?'

Chapter Thirteen

Alex turned the key in the ignition, and the van lurched forward and stalled.

'Sorry about that,' he apologised to his passengers. 'Perhaps you could advise me, Professor, as to how exactly one gets a van to move?'

The Professor gathered his thoughts. He really did not feel very well at all. His hands were shaking and there was no strength in his body.

'It's important, Professor,' urged Terry. 'We have to save the dodos from that evil man!'

The old man sighed, ran a hand over his face and nodded. 'Push in the clutch — that's the pedal to your left, Alex. Then you can engage the gears. Release the clutch and press on the accelerator pedal — on the right — and the van will move. The harder you press, the faster you go,' he explained as best he could.

Alex had to stretch his leg as far as he could to push in the clutch.

'Clutch engaged,' he announced.

'Now put the gearstick in first, and then turn on the engine.'

'Gearstick in first,' confirmed Alex, beginning to enjoy the lesson.

'Now turn the key, rev the engine and release the clutch.'

Alex turned the key. The engine fired into life. It was beautifully tuned. Alex took his left foot off the clutch and pushed the accelerator with his right. The van bounced forward and roared down the lane.

'Yippee!' shouted Terry.

Alex clutched the steering wheel. He had driven a dodgem car once, at a carnival, but his steering still needed some work. Thank goodness the fog had lifted.

Mildred 7 had kept her head low ever since the blue van had arrived in the yard. She knew what that van meant. Now, as it lurched and bounced down the lane, she cautiously emerged from her hiding-place behind one of the barns and resumed pecking at the walnuts which were strewn about the yard.

'Watch the gate, Alex!' shouted Terry, as the van, moving at a steady fifteen kilometres per hour, neared the gate of the estate.

'It's very narrow, isn't it?' said Alex nervously, and closed his eyes tightly.

Most of the van got through the gate, but the back bumper, unfortunately, got ripped off when it scraped a pillar.

'Well done, Alex! You're a born driver!' yelled Terry. The Professor stared wide-eyed ahead.

'I am, aren't I?' agreed Alex. He was getting quite excited. 'How do I make this thing go faster?'

'Isn't this fast enough?' asked the terrified Professor.

'No!' answered the twins together.

'Then put it in a higher gear.'

'Here goes,' shouted Alex, his eyes blazing. He slammed in the clutch and, with dreadful crunching noises, pushed and pulled the gear lever into second. The engine was screaming like a banshee with stomach pains.

'Hold onto your hats,' he called happily, releasing the clutch and pushing the accelerator all the way to the floor.

The van flew forward. The Professor and Terry were thrown back against their seats, their legs in the air. There was a great squeal of tyres and another squeal, one of pure joy, from Alex.

Terry glanced across at him. What had come over her prim and proper brother? Behind a wheel, he was a different boy.

'And now for third gear!' Alex cried, shoving in the clutch and struggling with the gearstick. He had trouble finding the gear this time, and the van was moving quite fast.

'Here, hold the wheel, Terry,' he ordered, 'while I sort out this gearstick.'

Terry had just enough time to stretch out a hand to the steering wheel before Alex let it go and grabbed the gearstick with both hands. It shuddered in his grip as he wrestled with it.

Terry did her best, leaning across the Professor and trying to steer with one hand; but the van was careering all over the narrow road.

A man on a bicycle was cycling slowly on what should have been his own side of the road. As the crazed blue van charged towards him, he leapt off his bike and into the ditch.

'Oh, I can't look!' cried Terry, as she drove straight over the bicycle. It got caught under the van, and they could hear it dragging along the road beneath them. The Professor had his eyes closed. He appeared to be mouthing prayers.

'Ah, to hell with third gear,' declared Alex. 'I'll put it straight into fourth!' He shoved the gearstick into fourth and, to Terry's relief, resumed steering the van.

The road to Narrowview is mostly narrow and winding. Fortunately, it is also very quiet. Its one and only straight stretch is as you approach the level crossing. This allows you plenty of time to stop if a train is coming. Being on a small road, the crossing is marked only by a single wooden barrier, which is lowered as the train approaches.

The van — now rather battered — was zooming towards the crossing at top speed. Its driver could barely see out over the steering wheel and had no idea how to stop the vehicle which he was driving with such abandon.

'Alex, the barrier is down!' shrieked Terry. 'There's a train coming! Stop the van!'

Alex had not thought of that. Professor Miller's instructions hadn't included advice on stopping.

'I don't know how to!' He turned his gaze to the old man. At once the van veered to the side of the road, and the beautifully polished wing-mirror on Alex's side made sickening contact with a road sign for the level crossing.

Alex rapidly brought the van back to its original course, heading straight down the middle of the road. The level crossing was getting closer and closer.

'Professor! Professor, how do you stop the van?' cried Terry, shaking the poor man. He sat petrified and dumbstruck. He was not enjoying the ride.

'I can't remember!' he shouted hysterically, suddenly opening his eyes and staring wildly about him.

They were approaching the junction fast. And so was the express train. Its great engine thundered along the track.

'Don't worry, I can handle this,' Alex told his terrified passengers. He slammed the accelerator to the floor.

The engine of the van, so sweetly tuned, so lovingly cared for by Sam Biddle, responded immediately: the van powered forward, smashing through the wooden barrier of the level crossing and out on the other side — beating the train by a hair's breadth.

'Yo!' shouted Alex. 'This is living!'

Terry felt the blood draining from her face. She thought she might get sick. The Professor was squeezing her hand so tightly it hurt.

Alex was having the time of his life. All those years of caution, those years of watching his every step, of calculating, of reasoning, of ordering, of self-discipline and self-control, were cast away, out the window! This was a new Alex bursting from his cocoon — born to drive, born to rescue dodos!

The signpost said 'Narrowview 9 km' before Alex clipped it with the side of the van and sent it headlong into a ditch. The damage to Biddle's once-immaculate van was yet another long dent along its left side panel.

'We'd better hurry,' said Terry, glancing at her watch. The other wing-mirror went skywards as Alex grazed a lamppost. 'It's almost six.'

Alex thought quickly. The shortest distance between two points is a straight line. The straightest, and therefore shortest, distance between where they were and Narrowview was through the next field on the right.

'This might be a little bumpy,' he warned the Professor, who seemed to be trying to crawl under the seat. Then he swung the van through the open gate and into the field.

This detour was to prove most fortunate. An articulated lorry, which took up most of the road, almost immediately appeared from around the next bend. Even a driver of Alex's ability would have found it

NARROWVIEW 9KM

impossible to avoid a head-on collision while travelling at such a high speed.

Meanwhile, Alex, Terry and the Professor were bumping about in the van as it lurched across the field.

It must be said that Rags really enjoyed this stage of the journey. To the brave little dog, the drive across the field was a roller-coaster ride — he never knew in which direction his spread-eagled body would be sent skidding and sliding next. It had been a wonderful day

— he had bitten Biddle's bum, and now he was being rewarded with this glorious drive, slip-sliding about the back of the van .... Oh, truly, Rags had never known such riches!

Terry thought that all of her teeth would be shaken out of her head, and the Professor's spectacles were bouncing up and down on his nose.

'It's like a rodeo!' laughed Alex. 'Biddle's van is the bucking bronco — but have no fear, I'll break it in!'

'I'm sure you will,' agreed Terry. 'I think the back wheels are going to fall off.'

'How do you propose to get out of this field?' enquired the Professor, who seemed to be pulling himself together.

The old man had a point. There was no gate at the far side of the field, and the van was hurtling drunkenly towards a stone wall.

'Good point, Professor,' Alex shouted back, making no attempt to slow down, 'but fear not. I have a plan.'

'Oh, dear,' muttered the Professor. 'I was afraid of that.'

Alex had spotted an old two-wheeled cart resting against the wall. It was tipped back on its end, its tailgate open. It had obviously been there for a long time; the van's headlights picked out long grass growing over its wheels. It was going to be the makeshift ramp which Alex hoped would get them over the wall and onto the main road, a mere hundred metres from Narrowview.

'Hold on tight!' cried Alex, as the van raced up the ramp.

Rags, with a yelp of pure joy, slid down the length of the van and crashed against its doors.

Terry couldn't look. The Professor's eyes nearly popped out. Alex clutched the steering wheel as the van flew through the air, clearing the wall and a wide ditch on the far side, and landed with a bone-wrenching thump in the middle of the road. Its four wheels splayed outwards, and great jagged cracks flung themselves all over the windscreen.

'The Eagle has landed!' yelled Alex. 'Next stop the airstrip!'

The blue van waddled forward. Its four duck-footed wheels all seemed to want to go in different directions, and its hopelessly cracked windscreen made it very difficult to see where they were going.

It had been market day in Narrowview, and the tired hawkers and stallholders were taking down their stands and packing up their wares. Alex helped them. The van veered down the main street, knocking down stands and stalls like ninepins, sending their owners fleeing for safety.

'We're going to have some explaining to do,' muttered Terry, as a box of cauliflowers went flying all over the road.

By the time Biddle's blue van left the main street, the place looked like the set of a war movie. Its shell-shocked shoppers and shopkeepers looked about in total bewilderment at the shambles that Alex had made of the street.

'The next left, Alex,' instructed the Professor, who was definitely rallying.

The van wobbled down a lane to the left. It was in a sorry state; its former glory was only a memory. It limped sadly down the rutted track; then, with a final shudder, its back axle gave up the ghost and it collapsed in front of a low, wide red barn. Its engine sputtered and stalled.

Sam Biddle's once-smart, once-beautiful blue van had reached its final resting place.

Chapter Fourteen

The red barn lay at the very edge of the airfield. It was occasionally used as a hangar for maintenance work on the few aircraft that used the airstrip. However, Narrowview Airfield was not a busy place, so most of the time a local farmer used the barn as just that — a barn.

The twins and the Professor did not know that it had recently been hired by a foreign gentleman. But they were about to find out.

They climbed the ditch from the road into the airfield. Professor Miller seemed to have recovered from his ordeal.

'Your driving appears to have loosened me up a bit!' he joked to Alex.

'Oh ... right,' mumbled Alex. Terry snorted behind her hand.

The grass was long at this neglected end of the airfield. It was also very damp after the hours of fog and mist. Rags bounded through the wet grass with obvious pleasure; the Professor and the twins, however, were glad of their boots as they trudged through the deep tussocks towards the barn.

Dusk had given way to night, and the building was only a large dim shape in the enveloping darkness. There was no opening in the side of the barn they were

approaching — no door, no window, no light. They
held their hands out for fear of bumping into something in the dark.

At last their hands touched the corrugated metal
walls of the barn. They were cold and damp to the
touch. The old man and the children moved along,
allowing the wall to guide them first to one corner of
the building, then to another.

When they turned the second corner they saw the
plane. It stood, dark and sleek, on the cracked concrete
paving which ran from the barn to the runway. Beads
of water hung on its wings and body. A drop of water
gathered, rolled along one of its long curved propellers,
and dropped silently to the ground. They could see the
shine running along the elegant body of the aircraft ....

They could see!

A thin shaft of yellowish light was escaping from a
partially boarded-up window at the other end of the
barn.

'It appears we've come to the right place,' whispered
the Professor. 'You two stay here. I'll go in and see
what's going on.'

Alex shook his head. 'We go in together,' he said.
Terry nodded.

Sighing in resignation, and a little relief, the old man
nodded and began to edge along the third wall of the
barn. The twins followed. They came to a large sliding
door, big enough to allow small planes into the building — and certainly big enough for a car and trailer.

The door was open a body's width. Rags began to
growl quietly, deep down in his throat. Terry put her
hand gently but firmly on his muzzle to quieten him.

One by one, stepping as carefully as they could so
that their rubber-booted feet would make no noise,

they went through the gap in the doorway.

The inside of the barn was dimly lit. There was a light-bulb shining at one end of it, but some large object blocked out most of the light. Still, after the darkness outside, even this gloom was an improvement.

No one made a sound. They knew that the crazy Marcel La Bouche had to be there somewhere — perhaps behind that large thing. They squinted at it, trying to make out what it was — some kind of machine, maybe .... Then Terry tugged at Alex's sleeve and pointed to another corner of the barn. Alex and the Professor turned to look.

It was the car! The large trailer was still hitched behind it. Hardly daring to breathe, the three of them moved gingerly towards the trailer.

The back of it was closed. Terry put her ear to the side of the trailer, and had to stop herself from shouting. She could just make out the odd scratch, the occasional cooing sound, from within. The dodos were still alive!

Terry beamed at the other two and gave them a quick thumbs-up. The Professor's shoulders sagged with sheer relief.

Alex pointed at his sister and the Professor.

'Open the doorway — I'll start the car — you jump in — and off we go!'

But there was no time to carry out this plan. There was a groaning, creaking sound and then a thud. The barn door had been closed.

A strong light was turned on with a loud click. The three of them froze where they stood, too frightened and dazzled to move. Rags barked.

From the shadows behind the barn door emerged the tall figure of Marcel La Bouche. His crisp tailor-made suit outlined his dark, menacing shape. His elegant black leather shoes made a loud, slow clicking noise as he stepped deliberately and mockingly towards them. He had an ugly sneer on his face — and an even uglier gun in his hands. It was pointed at them.

'So, Professor Miller,' he purred, 'you and your little friends have proven very clever.'

He paused and smiled. 'But, alas, not clever enough.' He gestured with his gun. 'How do you say? Ah, yes ... I hold the winning card.' He laughed.

'Let the children go,' pleaded the Professor, with his hands up.

'But no. I cannot. You are all my guests now. Yes?' Marcel's false, charming smile faded into an icy stare. 'You will all stay.'

It was not an invitation they could refuse.

The world's most famous chef gestured towards the large machine at the other end of the barn.

'Move over there. Now!'

Hands raised, the three walked over towards the machine. Terry dragged Rags by the collar.

'This is far enough,' La Bouche barked. Then his tone of voice changed again.

'So, you managed to defeat poor old Biddle, eh? Well, no matter. This was to be his last job for me anyway.

'It means that I shall have to do the work myself, but no matter. This was to be Biddle's last day — so to speak. He was a fool to think I would share anything with him.'

He looked at the gun.

'I was going to — how you say? — *retire* him. Yes ... retire him. Now I shall not have that unpleasant task. I must thank you all. You have saved me some bother, yes?'

The three stared at the madman, petrified.

'This is madness!' exclaimed the Professor.

'No, old man!' snapped Marcel La Bouche. 'This is business. I have hundreds of clients who will pay me ridiculous amounts of money to cook your precious birds for them. These dodos will be my finest meal, my masterpiece. And I have you to thank.' He gave the Professor a mocking bow.

'I will also become very, very rich,' he added.

Marcel strode purposefully over to a panel at the side of the machine. He pressed a series of buttons, and the machine began to come to life.

And what a machine it was! None of the three knew what it did, but it had the same dark air of evil as Marcel.

It was huge. Black. It looked like a gigantic dark caravan. Large ribbed pipelines, dozens of them, looped and twisted along its sides. They made the machine look alive. Thinner cables, the thickness of hosepipes, coiled around the pipelines and plugged into the sides of the machine.

Deep inside the machine, a sucking, gurgling noise could be heard. Every few seconds it gave a gasping wheeze, followed by a loud humming.

'It takes a little time to warm up,' explained Marcel, as though he were making excuses for some wayward child.

Orange lights began to flash. A large door opened at one end of the dark mechanical monster. Marcel quickly stepped away from it.

A small bell rang.

DING!

'Ah, it is ready!' beamed Marcel, as if a kettle had just come to the boil.

With an electric hum, a conveyor belt slid out of the doorway in the front of the machine. The conveyor belt was moving steadily. Anything placed on it would be swiftly drawn through the doorway and into the machine itself. There was a smell of oil and electricity.

'What is that thing?' asked Alex. He had a strong suspicion that it wouldn't be anything nice.

'This, my friend, is ... the Machine!' declared Marcel La Bouche.

The old man and the two children stared at him, mystified.

'Ah ... I see that you do not understand,' purred Marcel smugly. 'Perhaps I should give you its full name. It is the Plucking and Sucking Machine!'

Professor Miller's face went pale with horrified understanding.

'You mean — it's ...?' Words failed him.

'Yes, old man. You have guessed it,' smirked La Bouche. 'It's going to, ah ... *process* — yes, that is it — process your birds for me.'

'You're mad,' the Professor half-whispered.

'I'm not interested in your opinions, you old fool!' snapped Marcel. His charm had evaporated. He didn't like being called mad.

'Keep those brats under control,' he ordered, pointing the gun into their faces. 'Do not move or you will regret it.'

Still pointing the gun at them, he backed away towards the trailer and fumbled behind him for the latch which opened the tailgate. He kept his eyes, and the gun, on them all the time.

'You will be very useful to me,' he called to them. 'When your feathered friends see you, they will go straight to you — and to the Machine.'

'He's right,' hissed Terry. 'The poor things will come straight to us.'

'Say nothing,' whispered the Professor. 'We have to try to buy more time.'

Marcel had opened the latch on the trailer's tailgate. It lowered itself gently, on springs, like a drawbridge. The dodos stirred in the light and began to wander down the tailgate, totally unaware of the danger they were in.

'You see,' crowed the delighted Marcel, 'they recognise their old friends. They are going to you.'

Sure enough, the dodos, all fifty-four of them, had started to wander towards the three horrified onlookers. Marcel followed, his expensive shoes once again making their deliberate, menacing clicking sound as he approached.

The Plucking and Sucking Machine made some more gurgling, guzzling noises — as if it knew there would be work to be done, very soon.

The dodos crowded around their three human friends. They seemed totally at ease. Marcel had moved back near the conveyor belt.

'Let me see ....' He fingered some switches and dials on a control panel beside the conveyor belt. 'Your — ah, *my* birds each weigh between twenty and twenty-five kilos, yes? I will set the Machine to operate on bodies of that weight. Mistakes could be disastrous,' he confided.

Alex felt a gentle tugging at his foot. It was Dotty, the dodo with a fondness for shoelaces. She was idly inspecting his rubber boots. Disappointed, she wandered away from him to inspect Terry's feet.

'Once I set the plucking and sucking programme in motion, nothing can stop it,' declared Marcel La Bouche.

Dotty turned from Terry's booted feet in disgust. Still, there was always the Professor.

'My marvellous Machine will turn the birds into dodo fillets and dodo drumsticks in no time,' Marcel continued.

'What does your diabolical Machine do, exactly?' asked the Professor. He was grimly trying to buy time, in the hope that some miracle would save them. He could feel Dotty pecking at his boot. A lump rose in his throat. All his work, all the years — all wasted by this madman.

'Of course, you would want to know!' Marcel was delighted to have a chance to show off. Dotty had spotted his beautiful, handmade, black leather shoes.

'Once the bird is put on the conveyor belt, it is whisked into the first chamber of the Machine,' Marcel began his lecture.

Dotty's marvellous bottle-opener beak untied the lace of one shoe.

'Here, the first part of the process takes place — that is the plucking.'

The second shoelace was open.

'It might even tickle a bit!' joked the madman with the gun.

Now for the bit that Dotty liked. She quietly picked up one end of the first shoelace and laid it over an end of the second.

'B-but don't you ... put the birds out of their misery first?' stammered the Professor.

'It wastes too much time,' answered Marcel.

Loop the first bit around the second bit. Draw it gently. Dotty's beak worked carefully. This was great fun!

The twins' eyes were locked on La Bouche's feet. He ignored them. He was warming up to his lecture.

'The second part of the process is vital,' he said. 'Any mistake in setting the weight could cause an overload!'

'Could that happen now?' asked Alex hopefully.

'No, no, no.' The lunatic frowned in irritation at the idea. 'I have set the Machine to the proper weights. Now, do not interrupt me.'

Reach for the other bit from the first shoelace and pull it across ....

'Anyway, where was I? Ah, yes. The sucking process is ingenious, I think you will agree. The plucked bird is moved into the second chamber, where sharpened tubes are pushed into the body.'

Put *that* shoelace over *there* ....

'Then the pump sucks out the insides from the body — very quickly. That is why it is called the Plucking and Sucking Machine — you see?'

Professor Miller's face was a picture of horror and revulsion.

'You do this while the bird is still alive?' he gasped.

'Well ....' Marcel scratched his head. 'I would imagine that death comes fairly soon after that.'

Fighting back his anger and disgust, the Professor said nothing. He could see Dotty quietly working away on the madman's shoes. Perhaps if he were to trip, the twins might manage to escape before he could catch them. Time — they needed time!

'Then what happens?' he asked.

'After the sucking, the carcass is moved into the third chamber, where it is cut into pieces and packed into plastic bags. I always use the best quality bags, you know,' La Bouche assured them.

There, that was a pretty good knot. Dotty was pleased with herself. She hadn't had a good pair of shoelaces to tie up in ages ....

'But enough of this idle chatter,' said Marcel. 'I have work to do, and you will help me.'

'We will not!' shouted Terry angrily.

Marcel looked at her coldly and pointed the gun straight at her. His hand reached out and pressed a large red button beside the doorway to the Machine. The conveyor belt kept on rolling.

Marcel spoke in clear, icy tones.

'You, old man and little boy, begin putting the dodos on the conveyor belt. One by one, when I tell you to.'

'And if I refuse?' Alex's voice trembled.

'Then I will shoot your sister,' Marcel said. He sounded as though he meant it.

'All right. We will do whatever you ask.' Professor Miller's voice was shaking. 'But don't harm the girl.'

He knew that they would have only one chance of escape. Best keep it simple.

'At least give us room to work,' he said.

'But of course,' crooned Marcel. He was, after all, a gentleman. Keeping his eyes and his gun aimed at Terry, he took a step sideways ....

Then he tripped and fell flat on his face. The gun clattered across the concrete floor.

'Right! Let's go!' roared the Professor.

But before they could go any further than the barn door, they realised that something rather interesting — and quite dreadful — was happening to their enemy.

Marcel had fallen right over. Cursing, he had started to pick himself up off the ground and look for his gun. Unfortunately for him, he had not been paying attention to how close he was to the Machine.

The tail of his elegant jacket had become snagged in the conveyor belt. He was being pulled towards the Plucking and Sucking Machine.

Marcel's frown of annoyance became a gape of alarm.

He began to tug frantically at the tail of his jacket, hoping it would tear. No fear of that. Marcel always bought the best for himself; this was good-quality cloth. The conveyor belt drew him closer to the yawning mouth of his terrible invention.

'Try to take your jacket off!' yelled the Professor, as Marcel backed nearer to the Machine.

Alas, Marcel always buttoned his jacket up; he wouldn't be seen dead with it open! And, because of the pull of the conveyor, the buttons were too tight to open. Marcel was engaged in a desperate tug-of-war with the Machine. The Machine was winning.

He fought for a foothold, but the fact that his shoes were tied together probably didn't help. The Plucking and Sucking Machine hummed and roared loudly as it worked to pull in its victim.

Suddenly Marcel lost his grip. He was yanked backwards onto the conveyor belt, in a sitting position. The Plucking and Sucking Machine greedily drew him in.

As he disappeared backwards to his doom, the world's greatest soon-to-be-plucked-and-sucked chef raised his hand, pointing a finger as though he was about to say something; seemed to change his mind; shrugged; and vanished.

There was a whirring noise ....

'Yoooo! Hee hee hee — Ow! Ow ow ow!'

Plucked.

Then a loud guzzling, sucking noise ....

'Yeeeeeeeaaaaaaah!!'

Sucked.

And Marcel La Bouche was individually wrapped in fifty bags of the finest quality plastic.

However, Marcel had weighed a lot more than twenty-five kilos. The weight settings were wrong!

The Plucking and Sucking Machine's finely tuned balance was very seriously upset.

Pipes burst.

Motors overheated.

Sparks began to fly.

The whole Machine began to rock and shake violently. The dodos fled from it, towards the barn doors, which the Professor and the twins were opening as quickly as they could.

'Get them out fast!' shouted Professor Miller, over the incredible racket being made by the dying Plucking and Sucking Machine.

Chapter Fifteen

The twins and the Professor closed the barn door as quickly as possible. Smoke was beginning to sift its way out through gaps and cracks in the roof. Cracking and popping sounds could be heard inside. A flickering light danced on the wet grass below the barn's window. Soon the whole building would be an inferno.

The dodos huddled together in an anxious flock on the cracked pavement, near the sleek plane which had belonged to the late Marcel La Bouche. It would be a long and difficult task to lead the whole flock back to the Professor's house without being spotted by anyone. Very soon, the blazing barn behind them would be attracting a lot of unwanted attention. There were probably only a few minutes left before someone saw the flames and raised the alarm.

It would be difficult, to say the least, to explain how the fire had started. The presence of the dodos would also be extremely tricky to bluff away. And even if they managed all that, the discovery of a plucked, sucked, filleted and packaged Marcel La Bouche inside the wreckage of the barn would cause impossible problems. In short, it was time to hop it.

The twins glanced anxiously at each other. The Professor seemed to be deep in thought. Suddenly he clapped his hands and rubbed them together.

'There's only one thing to do,' he announced, 'and we've got to move quickly.'

With surprising speed, he strode over to the tail of the parked aircraft. He reached up, opened a door and climbed in.

'Right,' he called down to the twins, 'begin passing the birds up to me — gently, but quickly!'

As Terry passed the first bird up to the old man's waiting arms, a thought struck her.

'This isn't a good idea,' she panted (the dodo was heavy). 'Someone's bound to look inside the plane.'

'Nobody will look inside this plane,' Professor Miller grunted, lifting the second bird from Alex's arms. 'It won't be here.'

The twins nearly dropped the dodos they were carrying.

'Eh?'

'The plane won't be here,' repeated the Professor. 'Neither will the birds, and neither will I.' He lifted another dodo into the aircraft.

'You're not going to fly this thing,' gasped Terry. She and Alex had a rhythm going, lifting and carrying the now-peaceful birds. Half of them were aboard the plane. 'Are you?'

'Of course I'm going to fly it,' answered the old man. 'It's the only thing to do in the circumstances.'

'But it's ... it's ... it's complicated!' blurted Alex. He had to poke his head in through the doorway to call to the Professor, who had made his way forward to the cockpit.

'Keep loading the birds!' Professor Miller called back over his shoulder.

The twins looked at each other, shrugged, and continued their work. The dodos weighed a lot, and the children's arms ached with the effort of lifting and carrying them. Alex gestured to Terry; she nodded and pulled herself into the plane, and Alex started passing the remaining birds up to her.

Part of the barn roof collapsed in a shower of sparks. There wasn't much time left.

At least the Professor seemed to be having some success with the plane. The engine on the far wing made a loud humming noise, which increased to a deafening whine. The propeller twitched. Then the engine coughed into life. Instantly, the propeller started spinning, making a noise like an incredibly loud snore. The dodos flapped their stubby wings in panic at the noise; but, amazingly, within moments they had settled down again, reassured by the presence of their human friends.

The last dodos, Dotty and her chick, were lifted up to join their companions. Fortunately, all of the seats had been removed, so there was enough standing room for the birds. The twins jumped down to the ground, and the Professor made his way back to the doorway.

'Are you sure you can do this?' yelled Alex.

'Well, you did a marvellous job with that van of Biddle's, didn't you?' smiled the Professor.

'S'pose so,' admitted Alex uncertainly, remembering the steaming, battered wreck of the once-immaculate blue van.

'Well, there you have it. Same thing!' said the Professor.

He looked at the two white faces peering up at him.

'Don't worry!' he laughed. 'I've got a pilot's licence. I learned to fly years ago!'

The twins' shoulders sagged with relief.

'You have to be pretty versatile if you plan to raise dodos!' the Professor said with a wink.

Terry and Alex laughed nervously.

Flames were rising high from the barn. The alarm must surely have been raised. Time was precious, and very, very short.

Professor Miller beckoned, and the twins stood on tiptoe to raise their faces as near as possible to the old man who knelt in the doorway of the plane. It was a hard moment for all three of them.

'I've got to go,' the Professor said.

'But where?' asked Terry.

'To Miller Island,' he answered. 'This plane has been fuelled up for a long flight — maybe that maniac planned to fly as far as America. Anyway, I've enough fuel to get to the island.'

'What'll you do?' shouted Alex, over the roar of the engine.

'It's time to set the dodos free!' the Professor answered. 'There are enough of them now that they will have a real chance of surviving in the wild. Their numbers should increase.'

'Oh, I hope!' shouted Terry.

'It's up to the dodos now,' Professor Miller said. He looked sad. 'I want to tell you so many things — but there isn't time.' He leaned down to hug them both. 'But you will hear from me.'

'Promise?'

The Professor nodded.

'Stand back, now. I'd best get away before anyone arrives.'

He closed the door of the aircraft. Within a minute, the second engine had thundered up to full power; and moments later, the sleek plane began to move towards the runway.

Alex and Terry stood, arms around each other, as the plane carrying the world's only dodos and one kind old man zoomed off into the night sky. Soon its flashing tail-light had vanished into the night clouds.

And other flashing lights were approaching — blue ones. Neither of the twins wanted to stay around and explain what had happened. Anyway, who would believe them?

'C'mon, Rags!' shouted Terry, as they ran through the long wet grass towards home.

Chapter Sixteen

I t wasn't long before the police arrived to investigate
the burning of the barn at the airfield. They found
the crashed remains of a blue van nearby. There had
been complaints from Narrowview street-traders about
that same blue van driving in a very dangerous manner.

The next morning, tyre tracks were found outside
Professor Miller's home. The tracks matched the tyres
of the blue van. Very suspicious!

When the police investigated the house, they discovered that it had been broken into. One young officer
heard a muffled thumping coming from the cellar.

Shortly afterwards, a battered, overheated, dehydrated
and hysterical Sam Biddle was freed from some sort of
hot press which he'd managed to lock himself into.

'Do you admit to burning down the airfield barn?'
demanded a stern-faced police inspector.

'Dodos!' gasped Sam Biddle.

'Do you admit that you drove dangerously through
Narrowview village yesterday evening?'

'Dodos!' insisted the hysterical Biddle.

'What about breaking into this house?' the inspector
asked.

'Dodos! Dodos! Dodos!' yelled Biddle.

As they put the handcuffs onto his wrists, the inspector
wasn't sure whether Sam Biddle would be going to

prison or to an asylum.

But he would definitely be going somewhere.

'That guy is for the birds!' the inspector muttered to his sergeant. The sergeant nodded in agreement.

Two weeks later, an exciting and unexpected letter in a brown envelope arrived at the Hooray Henery Chicken Farm.

Grimm, Grimace and Snigger
Attorneys-at-Law
Narrowview.

Let it be known:

That Professor Aidan Miller of Miller House, Narrowview, has left all of his lands, properties, belongings and money in the care of Mr Alex Patterson and Miss Terry Patterson, of the Hooray Henery Chicken Farm, to be used as they see fit.

'Wow ....' whispered Alex.

'We could turn the estate into a holiday camp for battery hens!' suggested Terry.

'And an institute for research into endangered species of bird life!' cried Alex.

'And a shelter for stray dogs!' shouted Terry, jumping up and down and waving the letter about like a flag.

'Or a top-class restaurant specialising in my egg creations!' piped up Mrs Patterson.

'Now you're talking, lovey!' agreed Mr Patterson, and Rags went wild with excitement.

'Never!' yelled the horrified twins — and, to their

relief, both their parents burst out laughing.

Luckily for the twins, Mrs Patterson had other plans. She intended to write a book. And she did. *Mother Patterson's Egg Recipes* became a bestseller among dog-lovers all over the country.

As for Mr Patterson — well, he hasn't quite fixed that tractor yet; but he's working on it ....

In time, Alex and Terry turned Professor Miller's place into a haven for old, sick and endangered animals. 'Miller's Animal Sanctuary' offered a friendly and happy (if somewhat noisy) home to animals that had been treated cruelly, or that faced extinction, or that had simply outlived their usefulness. Terry, of course, gave every animal a name, and Alex gave them each a number.

One wily old bird rarely seen about the sanctuary was Mildred 7. She never returned to the Hooray Henery Chicken Farm. At first she missed her dodo friends, especially Dotty, but as time passed, Mildred 7 discovered that she quite liked her independence. The twins saw less and less of her. She had become Narrowview's first wild chicken.

Occasionally, the odd camper or hitch-hiker would tell tales of a strange bird who stared at them, unflinching and unafraid, on some lonely stretch of road in the surrounding countryside. Never again would she be afraid of Biddle — or of anyone else. Mildred 7 had answered the call of the wild.

The mysterious disappearance of the world-famous chef Marcel La Bouche was reported in all the papers. Although there have been several alleged sightings of him in far-flung corners of the world, none has as yet been confirmed.

And what of Professor Miller and his dodos?
    What, indeed!

More Amazing best-sellers by Jim Halligan and John Newman

FOWL DEEDS

Kate and Simon think they're going on holiday with their mother.
Then, when her maniac boss Ollie Slycke of Krew-Doyle Petroleum makes her go off searching for oil, they think they're struck in batty Great-aunt Florrie's semi-detached prison.

They never expect to find themselves on a tropical island with an eccentric old Professor, slimy Slycke, his scary sidekick Skellington, a lot of dynamite, a lot of surprises – and a lot of dodos.

ISBN: 0-86327-639-3

Even More Fantastic Best-sellers by Jim Halligan and John Newman

ROUND THE BEND

Under the new management of Harry, Liz and Tiny, the
E.C. Dussitt School of Motoring is in for a bumpy ride.
And to crunch the gears even further, thick Ron Locke
needs driving lessons to perfect his getaway expertise for a
big bank job.

With the help of confused Eddie, lovesick Larry and a
homemade car, Harry, Liz and Tiny must put the brakes on
the robbers' scheme!

ISBN: 0-86327-748-9

Coming soon from
Jim Halligan and John Newman...

Jim Halligan John Newman

SEEING RED

Ben Addle has a problem – he's colour-blind. When other
people see red, Ben sees green. This lands him in all kinds
of trouble especially with his sadistic teacher. Then Ben
discovers a strange box deep in a bog where a Druid lost it
5,000 years ago. With magic powers like these he thinks his
problems are over. Until he realises that there are red and
green lights coming out of the box.

What do the lights mean? How does the box work? Is it
dangerous? With the help of his sister Annie and his secret
pet pig Messy, Ben tries to find out. But they are not the
only ones who are interested in the box. When it falls into
the wrong hands the whole town is in danger. Ben has to try
to recover the box before it's too late...

ISBN: 0-86327-903-1

Also by Wolfhound Press

THE BLACK BAG MYSTERY
Richard Lysaght

Have you ever had a really bad year?
You know, like, one where something terrible happens
to your dog.
One where your Dad never stops biting your head off.
One where a suger-coated cousin from hell comes to
stay and makes your life an absolute misery.
One where you start trying to find out what's going on
in the woods.
One where you wish you'd never heard of a black bag.
You have?
Well then, you didn't have a really bad year; you had,
like me,
the worst year of your life.

ISBN: 0-86327-886-8